THE H1

BOOK ONE OF *THE TIME THIEF SERIES*

RICHARD A. SWINGLE

Illustrated by Janet Swingle

<u>LWP</u>

For all my friends across the seas, whose diverse cultures have inspired and made this Englishman feel welcome wherever he goes.

JOIN THE RICHARD A. SWINGLE READER GROUP

Sign up for the no-spam newsletter and get exclusive content, behind the scenes insights to the writing process and advance information about forthcoming titles.

There will also be the opportunity to join the Richard A. Swingle advance reader tribe, which opens up to applications a couple of times a year. There you'll have the chance to receive free review copies of books pre-publication.

Visit: www.richardaswingle.com to sign up now.

1

Ilaria turned and ran from the muddy swamp; her heart pounding, her legs numb as she willed them not to give up on her. She had reclaimed the dragon's heart from the creature. A heart thief from an ancient tribe of underground dwellers. Ilaria couldn't believe she had got this far but now she had to escape and she hadn't thought to plan that far ahead.

She heard the creature's screams as it chased her. It was desperate to find her but she was so small, just eleven years old.

Ilaria managed to tuck herself amongst the roots of a large upturned oak tree that had been blown over in a storm, its roots jutting out like tentacles. She lay there hiding for what seemed like an age though it was barely a smattering of moments.

What are you doing, Ila? she asked herself. *What on earth are you doing here?*

The forest went quiet and still, not even a whisper of a

breeze. Ilaria knew she needed to move. She had to make it back to the cave and return the heart to the dragon or her wish would never be granted.

She opened the rolled-up cloth that held the heart, fearful that she had imagined obtaining it. But there it was, less like a heart and more like a stone. It glowed a deep shade of green, pulsating as though it had never ceased beating. She wrapped it up again before turning to run from her hiding place.

Sometime later, Ilaria managed to sneak her way out of the forest, back to the sunken cave that was hidden beneath a grassy bank, the entrance lined with an honour guard of bare-branched olive trees.

She hurried inside and grabbed a flaming torch from an old hook on the wall. The same one she had used to find the dragon the first time.

There he was, sleeping inside an alcove at the back of the cave. Though injured and weak, she could still feel the force of the air as his breath rushed past her. Ilaria pulled back the thick hessian rags that covered the wound from where the heart had been taken.

She placed it back inside. It was a messy business and she felt the muscles inside the dragon clamp hold of her arm, massaging the heart back into its rightful place. Ilaria tugged her arm away and flicked the smelly viscous gore off at once. The dragon roared and a bright light filled his eyes as he lifted his head.

'Run child, run. You must run NOW!'

Ilaria didn't wait to understand why, for the dragon had guided her this far. She used what energy she had remaining and fled through the cave as the roaring sounds of the dragon advanced upon her. She felt a sudden wave of heat on her back that was almost blistering and she dived through the cave mouth, taking shelter behind a rock.

A large flame burst out through the opening, singeing all the grass and turning the few remaining autumnal leaves to ashes. When the roaring stopped, Ilaria stood and waited as the dragon stomped forwards, his footsteps closing in on her. When he finally exited the cave, he seemed twice as large as when she had first found him.

'I'm impressed girl, I never thought you could do it,' bellowed the dragon.

Ilaria swallowed hard and found her reply.

'I've done as you asked, now please, you must save him.'

'Before I can grant you the wish, there is something you must know.'

'What is it? Tell me,' she pleaded.

The dragon sighed a guilty sigh.

'If I use my power to save your grandfather, my heart will be extinguished and I will die.'

Ilaria was stunned.

'What? How can you only be telling me this now? I did everything you asked of me. Risked my own life and…'

'I am sorry, child, but had you known, you never would have gone to such lengths. You needed to be focused.'

'Never would have gone to such lengths? I fell from my world into yours without a single idea as to why. I found you here, you told me you could save him.'

'And I meant it, child,' replied the dragon. 'The decision is yours and I cannot refuse you once you have made up your mind.'

Ilaria broke down in tears; this ordeal had been thrust

upon her and an olive branch extended, but it bore rotten fruit.

Life had been cruel to her before, especially when she had first found out that her grandfather was dying of cancer. She was still so young and he was her entire world, the only family she had ever known. Now she had to value his life more than the magnificent dragon.

Ilaria felt as though she had been tricked. *How could someone remain innocent if they choose to take a life?* she asked herself.

Ilaria took something out of her jacket; it was an old Italian gold florin that had been shaped to fit a chain that her grandfather had given her on her tenth birthday. It was the only thing she had ever owned that was once her grandmother's. She held it out to the dragon.

'This is for you to keep. As a reminder of the hope you once gave to a young child and of the grandfather you stole from her.'

Ilaria dropped the florin necklace on the ground and then turned and ran, crying and afraid. Her tears smeared across her face as she feared that it was too late, too late to return home and say goodbye. She fell to the ground exhausted, all the energy had gone from her body. She looked to the spiralling pathway before her and the world faded into a starry darkness.

WHEN ILARIA WOKE, she was back in the hole that she had fallen down. It was hidden amongst the sand dunes by the beach where she lived, ten feet deep and impossible to climb back out of. She couldn't remember how she had returned here but began to attempt to scramble out. It was hopeless.

'Johnny,' she called out. 'Johnny are you there?'

'Ila!' called the grubby boy. 'What on earth have you been doing down there? It was so dark and I couldn't see you so I went back to find a rope. Here.'

Johnny fed the rope down the hole just far enough for Ilaria to grab hold of. She tugged on it to check it was taut.

Johnny laughed at her. 'Don't worry, I'm not stupid, I tied it off to a bench.'

'A bench?' She sounded doubtful. Johnny wasn't the sharpest tool in the shed after all.

'Yes, it's cemented into the ground, just climb up already, will you?'

Ilaria grabbed hold of the rope and pulled herself up as much as she could whilst Johnny helped haul the rope higher. When they were close enough to each other he held out his hand and helped her safely out of the hole.

'You must have hit your head and blacked out, you were down there for hours,' said Johnny, concerned.

Ilaria shook her head and replied. 'I'm fine, don't worry.' She began to walk back along the sand dunes as the waves crashed beneath her. Johnny ran to catch up.

'You're not going to tell your grandfather about this, are you? I don't think he'll ever forgive me.'

'Go home, Johnny, nothing is going to happen to you.'

'Are you sure you're okay?'

'Yes, I just want to be left alone now, alright?'

Johnny sensed she was unsettled by something and knew not to pry further.

'I'll see you at school on Monday then.'

'Bye, Johnny,' Ilaria shouted as the coastal winds carried her voice off over the sea.

BY THE TIME Ilaria arrived home, a thin mist had filled the streets that led to her house. There wasn't a single soul to be seen in the eerie fog.

A fox running across the road startled her, banging its head on a wooden garden fence as it fled. She was amused to have been scared by such a small creature. But now fear took hold of her again as she approached the steps of her house. She turned the key in the lock, slowly and cautiously, making as little sound as she could.

After she slipped inside she noticed the hallway light was still on and she knew then that her grandfather was still awake. She felt a rush of relief and at the same time she was afraid at having returned home so late.

'Grandad,' she shouted. 'Are you still awake?'

There was no reply, though she had expected none. His hearing was not what it used to be. Ilaria had become accustomed to shouting her apologies into thin air. It was far easier than facing the stare of those weathered old eyes. Then, as she entered the living room she saw something she could not believe. Her grandfather was standing on a stool preparing the lights on a Christmas tree. She hadn't seen him out of his wheelchair for two months, except for when he slid in and out of bed.

'What are you doing?' she blurted out.

'Ilaria dear, what does it look like? It's just gone midnight and today is the first of December.'

'That's not what I meant. I thought you'd be in bed.'

'Ah, yes, perhaps I should be, but needs must.'

'What do you mean?' she asked.

'Pass me that, would you?' He pointed to the small table beside the tree and on it lay the old florin. The very chained necklace that she had left with the dragon lay there before her, shining brightly as it reflected the multicoloured lights of the Christmas tree.

Ilaria couldn't believe it. Had she dreamed meeting the dragon? She felt as though she had passed into a parallel universe and allowed herself to believe that her grandfather had never been ill at all.

She passed it to him and he smiled, holding her hand for a moment. Ilaria could have sworn he had winked at her with his crooked eyes as he hung the coin at the top of the tree. He grinned confidently. 'I think this year, Ila, we're going to have a very good Christmas indeed.'

2

S now painted the rooftops of the entire coastal village. Southbourne had never been blanketed by so much snow, especially on Christmas Day. It was a quiet little place on the outskirts of Bournemouth and at the foot of the New Forest where Ilaria Hope had spent her entire life. She was a very outdoorsy girl, with long dark hair and brown eyes, who loved to run amongst the trees, racing all the wild animals.

She had become used to entertaining herself from a very young age as her grandfather, who had raised her, often went away for work trips. Brian Hope had put off his retirement after Ilaria's parents and grandmother had been killed in a plane crash off the coast of Tuscany. Finances were tight and he relied heavily on their neighbours to take care of Ilaria when he was out of town. Ilaria had become very close to everyone in her local community.

Christmas Day was their chance to return the favour by cooking a huge lunch for them all. But little did Ilaria know that after this Christmas her life would change forever.

. . .

ILARIA AWOKE, excited as she always was on Christmas morning, and turned to look out of her window. She could barely believe her eyes as she saw the snow had piled up as high as the window, which was rather remarkable considering her bedroom was on the first floor.

She ran downstairs and into the living room to open the curtains and there before her stood a great big fluffy white wall. She jumped up and down with glee until a moment later the reality dawned on her.

'Oh no, we're trapped.'

'Yes. I am afraid we are,' said Brian, her grandfather, who looked remarkably well for someone who had been diagnosed with lung cancer a few months ago. He smiled down at Ilaria, amused at their predicament. Ilaria had become used to pushing him around in his wheelchair after it had become too painful for him to walk.

A physical struggle though it was, the awkwardness it made her feel was worse. They would pass other children her age that were out playing in the streets and often they would invite her to join in but she never could. She didn't mind. Ilaria loved her grandfather and there was nowhere she would rather be.

She had taken him to the local butcher's shop and grocery store in his wheelchair and even pushed him along the high street to the local barber to get a haircut while she waited patiently to take him home again. Thankfully, Southbourne was a relatively flat area.

It pained Ilaria that she wasn't strong enough to take him down the steep pathway to the beach. So, to see him walking around now, good as it made her feel, was confusing to say the least.

Ilaria thought about how she was likely to lose her grandfather at any moment and she wondered if his newfound health had anything to do with the day she had fallen into the hole by the coast.

Did I really meet the dragon? Was it a dream? Ilaria wasn't sure of the answer to either question. She had been far too afraid to speak to her grandfather about any of it. She wondered if he knew something but with the risk of sounding stupid, she was too afraid to ask.

'Well, Mrs Witt is going to be very disappointed about not getting her turkey leftovers this year,' said Brian.

'Grandad, surely we can still keep our lunch plans? There must be a way?'

'Don't be daft, hummingbird,'—Ilaria hated it when he called her that— 'we've got no chance of making it out of this house today.'

'I have an idea!' Ilaria shouted excitedly before running into the kitchen to pick up the phone. Brian stood there smiling at his granddaughter as she called the neighbours, blurting instructions at them down the telephone. She then hung up and ran upstairs to her bedroom and opened the window. A cold wave of air came in towards her and she shivered. Quickly, she grabbed a jumper and threw it on over her pyjamas.

After a couple of minutes of standing there with her curious grandfather at her side, a rope came swinging down over the top of the window and Ilaria ran to grab it. She pulled enough slack through to wrap it around a bedpost and then threw the rest of the rope back out of the window.

'Got it, Ilaria! Darling, you are a genius,' came the shrill, elderly voice of their neighbour, Mrs Witt.

Brian moved to the window and peered outside, waving to her where she was hanging out of her own window.

'Morning, Mrs Witt, Merry Christmas,' he said.

'Merry Christmas to you both too.'

Some hours later, the oven timer rang and it was time to carve the turkey. The snow outside had not melted one bit but, thanks to Ilaria's bright idea, they had connected as many of the neighbours houses together as possible with string, ropes and hanging baskets.

Ilaria loaded up a Christmas lunch into a basket for Mrs Witt, which also had enough food for the old man that lived on the other side of her house.

'Thank you, Ilaria!' Mrs Witt cried out.

'You're welcome.'

Ilaria and Brian finally sat down at the dinner table to enjoy their own meal together. Despite the fact there hadn't been enough money for presents again this year, Ilaria couldn't be happier. It really was a fabulous Christmas.

'You know, Ilaria. I have to tell you that you really are a remarkable girl.'

Ilaria blushed, she had never been good at receiving compliments.

'It wasn't a difficult idea to come up with in the end, Grandad,' she replied.

He gave her one of his cheeky winks.

'Grandad?' Ilaria sounded curiously nervous.

'Yes, hummingbird?'

She rolled her eyes. 'Oh please don't call me that, you know I hate it!'

'Sorry, dear, go on.'

'I know I ask you every year, but, could you tell me about them all again? Please?' She looked at her grandfather with insistent eyes. He gave her a warm smile before responding.

'I still remember the day you were born, like it was yesterday. Your mother couldn't stand your father's fussing so I took him to the pub and we had fish and chips and a pint of bitter. In the meantime, your grandmother kept her company and gave the nurses hell. One thing that runs in the family on your mother's side is that fiery Latin streak.'

'Am I like them at all?' Ilaria asked.

'You're more like them than you will ever know. You have your grandmother's beautiful long hair and your mother's sense of adventure. None of your silly old English grandfather's traits at all!'

'Well that's not true, Grandad. I must get my appetite from you at least!'

Brian laughed. 'Yes, I suppose you must have.'

Ilaria smiled at him. They shared the same smile too.

'What is it like? The town that Grandma was from?'

'San Casciano, a beautiful hilltop town in Tuscany amongst all the winemakers of Chianti, which reminds me.'

Brian pulled out a corkscrew and undid the wrapping on a bottle of red wine that had arrived in a small wooden case a week earlier. He pulled out the cork and poured himself a glass before adding a drop to a glass for Ilaria to taste.

'Just a tiny drop, until you are old enough. This was your mother's favourite wine, she very nearly married the winemaker at the villa where it is made, you know. Had it not been for your father we may have all been living there still.'

'But then I wouldn't be here?'

'Yes, I suppose you're right,' considered Brian as he held up his glass. 'Salute.'

'Buon Natale,' Ilaria said as they chinked their glasses together. 'I wish I remembered them.'

'I know, sweetheart, I know.'

They enjoyed their meal together, pulling their Christmas crackers to reveal the silly paper hats that they then put on, and which always made them laugh. Brian finished his last mouthful of wine, which gave him courage as he had been trying to say something to her for a while. He put down his knife and fork and took a deep breath.

'Ilaria, I must tell you something, something very important. Your grandmother would have wanted your mother to tell you one day, when the time was right. Passing from one generation to the next. It should have been many years from now,' he paused to reflect. 'But I am afraid you'll have to hear it from this old codger instead.'

Ilaria gulped, she was afraid of what he might say next.

'One day, you will have to carry a weight far greater than you can imagine,' he continued, 'and from a far younger age than it is at all fair to expect. You and I have both lost those we love, they were taken from us far too soon. I never knew how to care for your mother when she was born, so to inherit the responsibility of raising you when you were just one year old was hard for me.'

Brian took another pause, wiping away a tear from his eye and again inhaled deeply.

'Your grandmother would have been so proud of you, Ilaria. I'm sorry—no, it's too soon—we still have time.'

'Grandad, please tell me. You always do this. I'm old enough now. Please!'

'You'll finish the year at school and after your twelfth birthday, I promise. I promise I will tell you everything. Merry Christmas, Ila.'

Ilaria sighed as she knew that was all he was going to say for now. 'Merry Christmas, Grandad.'

3

The spring term of school started with a bang. Before Ilaria and Johnny even reached their first class they had gotten into a fight with a nasty piece of work who went by the name of *Scars*, though really his name was Scott. Ilaria had always thought Scars was a stupid name, anyway, seeing as he didn't even have any.

Scott had approached the two friends with his gang of mates and started making fun of Johnny, just because Johnny was a little bit different.

If there was one thing in the world Ilaria hated, it was stupid boys making fun of her friend just because he didn't look the same. She was overtaken by the same rage that she felt after every injustice bestowed upon her friend and ran straight over to Scott and punched him right in the face. Scott's friends all laughed as he stumbled sideways to the floor.

'Aha ha, Scotty, beaten by a girl!' one of them bellowed.

This was enough to enrage Scott who got to his feet and

instantly kicked Ilaria in the shins. She felt her legs go weak and stumbled to the floor but not before grabbing Scott's shirt and dragging him to the floor with her. Just as she was about to claw at Scott she felt a strong pair of hands pulling her away from the boy. It was Mr Hill, her favourite teacher.

'Ilaria, what on earth is the matter with you?' he said.

"They were bullying Johnny. It's not fair!'

'All three of you come with me, right now.'

Ilaria, Johnny and Scott followed Mr Hill to his classroom whilst the rest of Scott's gang dispersed, running off in different directions.

Inside the room, the three children stood side by side in silence as Mr Hill glared at them all. On the walls were various images of religious leaders: Buddha, Shiva, Jesus, and many others. Mr Hill was a religious studies teacher, but he always thought of himself as more of a philosopher. Unfortunately for him, philosophy was not something that was taught in this school and he had been warned many a time for diverging from the curriculum. He had often argued that certain rules were there to be broken so it was ironic now that he was the one enforcing them.

'You can't fight like that,' he yelled. 'Not just because of the rules here, but because it's not right to harm each other. You must learn to respect each other's differences.'

'But, sir, my dad told me his family shouldn't even be here, they're illegal,' Scott blurted out.

'Scott, silence! That is the most ridiculous thing I have ever heard. You can tell your father I'll be writing to him personally to invite him here and I'll explain all about how immigration in this country has worked for the last five hundred years.' He took a moment to pause to let that sink in. 'Johnny is your neighbour and a fellow pupil at this school and any thoughts you have to the contrary you can forget right now. Do you understand?'

'Yes, sir.'

'Good.' Mr Hill turned his attention to Ilaria. 'Ilaria, you can't attack people just because they have made you angry. You will find many reasons in this life to be mad at people but hitting them won't solve the problem. You have to learn to talk to those who disagree with you and make them understand your point of view.'

'But he is always horrible and pushing other kids around!'

'That doesn't justify what you did. If anything, by hitting Scott you have given him a reason to hit back again.' Mr Hill pointed to a quote written on the wall above his head. It read, *An eye for an eye makes the whole world blind.*

'Do you know who said that?' their teacher asked as the three children shook their heads. 'It was Mahatma Gandhi. Now, Ilaria and Scott, both of you are going to write me an assignment on Mahatma Gandhi and hand it in at the end of the week. Five hundred words each.'

'What? That's ridiculous,' Scott retorted.

'Let's make it one thousand words for you, Scott. I can make it two thousand if you feel like arguing again. No? Good.'

Johnny raised his hand. 'Sir, do I have to write about Gandhi?'

'No, Johnny, but I would like a private word with you. Ilaria, Scott, you can both go.'

Ilaria and Scott left the classroom together with their

heads hung low. Ilaria pulled the door closed and turned to find Scott staring right at her.

Scott smiled. 'Do you want to be in my gang?'

'What? Why would I want to do that?'

'You hit like a boy, that's why.'

Ilaria shook her head and walked away from Scott, fuming as she heard his laughter echoing down the corridor.

THE REST of the school term went from bad to worse for Ilaria, as she got in more and more fights, regardless of the lessons that Mr Hill had taught her. It hadn't taken long for Scott's parents to complain about the teacher after he had broken up the fight that day. Needless to say, Scott didn't write an assignment on Mahatma Gandhi, though Ilaria did, and for that she was eternally grateful to Mr Hill. For otherwise she never would have learnt about him and his fight to pacify people without using violence.

The problem for her was that Gandhi had eventually been killed whilst walking in a parade one day. And now, just for varying the content of the school curriculum again, Mr Hill had been called into a meeting to explain his constant disobedience.

Before the month was out, his room had been cleared and a replacement teacher had come in and changed all the pictures of varying faiths to just depictions of Christ.

The room seemed somewhat monotone compared to before; it was as if Mr Hill's open mind needed colour and now the room was grey. Ilaria decided then that there was no fair justice in the world of adults or children, so for now she would continue to break as many rules as she dared, without thinking at all about the consequences.

'ILARIA HOPE. COME HERE AT ONCE!' shouted her grandfather.

Brian was standing in the middle of the kitchen with a letter in his hand. She had never seen him so angry. She sheepishly walked towards the kitchen from the hall that seemed to have tripled in length in the last few moments.

'Look at me, please.'

Ilaria looked up into his eyes. She could feel her own eyes burning and her vision blurred as tears came to the surface.

'Would you like to explain this?'

She shook her head.

'Seven stitches just above his eye. You could have blinded the boy. You do realise that, don't you?'

'Well at least he's earnt his stupid name now,' Ilaria said under her breath.

'What was that?' Brian asked.

'I'm sorry, I don't know what's wrong with me. I just get so mad all the time.'

With a hint of pride Brian continued. 'I know you like to protect your friends from these bullies. But you can't keep doing this. You'll become the very thing you despise!' He took a breath. 'You've been suspended for two weeks. You are lucky they didn't expel you completely.'

Brian took a step closer to Ilaria and dropped the letter onto the table next to her. He opened his arms and gave her a big hug. She clung onto him and never wanted to let go. She felt so safe.

'I won't do it again, I promise.'

'I can't help but think this is all my fault. Maybe if I had told you certain things sooner.'

Brian took a step back from her and gazed into her eyes. 'Ilaria, I think you are going to need to sit down.'

4

Ilaria couldn't believe her ears. Her grandfather was telling her things she had always wanted to know. They sat and spoke for hours and Brian allowed her to ask as many questions as she wanted. He explained about a world of dragons that lived on an island off the coast of Italy.

'Oglasa Island was uninhabited and a perfect place for these creatures to dwell as it led to a series of underground caves where they slept. They had been there for thousands of years, breathing their fire and heating the centre of the earth,' he told her.

'When their population had grown beyond a dozen, the heat rose so fiercely in the earth's core that parts of the earth's surface spat out devastatingly hot lava, which created mountains we know as volcanoes and filled the sky with ash. The ash became so thick that the world was thrown into a winter that threatened to end human life.'

'It's a lot to take in, Grandad,' said Ilaria. 'So what happens if the dragons all die?'

'I'm sure that would be bad news as well,' said Brian. 'The earth's core would probably begin to cool. The important thing is to find the right balance. A special bond exists now between the dragons and a select few people. Those people are your ancestors, Ilaria.'

Ancestors. Ilaria considered the word. It carried a huge weight and the implications of hundreds if not thousands of years of people bonded with dragons rattled her brain.

'Can't we just ask the dragons not to breathe their fire?' she asked.

Brian shook his head. 'In a way, that is exactly what happened, but they must breathe their fire the way you and I must breathe the air that exists around us. The way some animals must live in the sea. The way the sun must rise and set each day. Before the bond was made, so much ash was thrown up into the air that the heat from the sun was blocked out.'

Brian went on to explain how Ilaria's ancestors, who had recognised the unsustainable damage being caused by the dragons, came together to tame them and asked for their help. 'It was then that the deep underground world had come into existence. It is within those tunnels, deep beneath the island, that the dragons retreated and calmed their natural rage, reducing the amount of fire that travelled deep towards the centre of the earth. They still live there today.'

'The dragons have two hearts,' Brian explained, 'and the second gifted them with various powers; to live for thousands of years, to withstand the heat of the centre of the earth and, not least, to communicate through telepathy. A fact discovered by the great ancestor of yours, who had once travelled to Oglasa Island to create a pact with the fiercest of all the dragons. This was how the sect of tamers was born. Each dragon connects his magic heart to a human's, and as that person becomes too old to cope anymore, they pass on the connection.'

'I met a dragon, Grandad. I never told you but I fell down a hole when I was out walking with Johnny along the beach and I found him in a cave,' Ilaria admitted.

'Yes, he told me. Speranza and I are bonded now. Though not in the same way that your grandmother was. He opened a pathway between you because he knew when I fell ill that our bond would eventually come to an end. Speranza was preparing you for this day it would seem. It is very tiresome to communicate with a dragon through telepathy. Do you recall waking that day with a headache?'

Ilaria nodded.

'Well, imagine that multiplied by a hundred times. You can only truly bond with a dragon by touching it, but you must carry a fragment of their second heart. Soon we must go to him.'

'So, I only dreamed of saving the dragon that day? But it felt so real.'

'In a way it was, at least the lesson was real. A dragon lives for thousands of years, unless their magic heart is stolen.'

Brian paused to check that Ilaria was still following him and he could see that she didn't understand. So he explained.

'You see, there is a group that live on the edge of the underworld who crave the power of the dragons for themselves. They are called *The Heart Thieves*. They are a race of creatures who hide beneath the surface, hunting the dragons in the network of caves that you dreamt about when you found our friend that day. It is said that language is lost to the heart thieves now. They were once not unlike humans but they were so selfish they eventually fought amongst themselves and dispersed, living in solitude.'

Ilaria remembered the creature she'd run from in her dream. She didn't like the idea at all that there was an entire tribe of these heart thieves living in the very caves where the dragons lived.

'I don't think I could cope with being bonded to a dragon.' Ilaria's nervous excitement betrayed her words.

'Ilaria, I am old and cannot continue the work that I inherited from your grandmother. It was never truly my destiny anyway. I am just a caretaker, but after your grandmother passed away so suddenly I had no choice. When I have taught you everything you need to know, we will travel to Tuscany to see him together and you will bond with him as I have done ever since that fateful day.'

Ilaria looked extremely confused, it was so much to take in. 'I'm sorry, Grandad, if I find this all a little hard to believe. It's just that, well, it *is* hard to believe.'

'Don't worry, hummingbird, tomorrow you will finally turn twelve years old and we begin your real schooling. I'll tell you all about our mutual friend. I will finally pass on the pendant that was meant for your mother. It contains the tiniest piece of the dragon's heart and it will bond you together, dragon and tamer,' Brian said proudly through his cheeky smile that Ilaria loved so much.

She had never felt afraid the way she did now. It was an odd sort of fear. The kind that comes the moment before you jump off a high diving board into a swimming pool. Her legs trembled as she saw herself plunging downwards with the world fading out around her. She just hoped that she would cope when she hit the water.

'What is his name?' Ilaria asked, hardly able to contain her anxiety.

'His name you know already,' said Brian. 'It is Speranza. It means Hope.'

5

Rain lashed through the window by Ilaria's bed. She had slept with the window wide open to cope with the early summer heat but the storm had come upon her without warning. She woke with a start, soaking wet, and ran to close the window. Her nightclothes were sodden, as were her bedsheets and everything else on her bedside table.

'Happy birthday, Ilaria,' she said with a frustrated whisper.

After a few minutes scurrying about to salvage her things, she managed to get into a dressing gown and brush her hair and finally felt ready for the day. It was still early and her grandfather would not be awake yet, so she decided to go downstairs and cook him his favourite breakfast: eggs Benedict with mushrooms and basil. He had told her many times how the lieutenant that he had served during the war would reward him with the meal every Friday morning. Brian only ever spoke to her about the war when he was recalling a fond memory. Though she knew there was also sadness from that time, a deep sadness that he would never share with her.

Once the eggs were ready, Ilaria dished up breakfast into two small dishes and carried them to the dining table beginning to get anxious about the food going cold. Grandad should have woken by now, she thought.

The smell of the fried mushrooms would usually be enough to rouse him. She took the plates back and put them in the oven on a low heat to keep them warm and went upstairs to her grandfather's bedroom. Ilaria knocked on the slightly ajar door and it crept open. No response came and the room inside was dark as the blinds were still drawn but Ilaria could see a heap lying on the floor beside the bed. She didn't have to run to him to know that he wasn't asleep. She didn't have to check for a pulse or a sign of breath. She knew it in that instant, as a shiver ran up her spine, that he was dead.

THE WHOLE SCENE had been a painful blur. A nightmare come to life. The paramedics tried everything to resuscitate Brian but it was hopeless. Ilaria, watched as they strapped an oxygen mask to his mouth and wheeled his body into an ambulance.

One of the paramedics tried CPR one last time but shook his head and threw a look filled with sadness towards Ilaria before closing the door.

'ILARIA, ILARIA HOPE. COME ON,' Ilaria finally became

aware of the voice that was calling to her. 'Let's get you into the car and we'll follow them to the hospital.'

The voice belonged to Johnny's mother, Nawal. She was a beautiful woman and, though fairly strict, she always knew how to smile and care for her son and his best friend. Ilaria hadn't known who else to call. Last time her grandfather had collapsed, he was still conscious and rang for the doctor himself. This time, Ilaria had rung Johnny's house in a panic and explained to Nawal what had happened.

Johnny had come over with his mother and the three of them left together, following the flashing blue lights of the ambulance to the hospital. It was the longest journey of Ilaria's young life.

Johnny looked over towards her but she remained silent, staring out of the car window as they went. He did the only thing he felt he could and took her hand in his own, feeling her squeeze it tight, as though clinging on for dear life.

When they arrived at the hospital, Ilaria saw her grandfather being wheeled out of the ambulance on a stretcher. A white sheet was completely covering his face and she knew that her silent prayers had been useless.

The following moments passed like a dream. Ilaria was consoled and given sympathies over and over. She listened to rambling sentiments of several nursing staff and the doctor who had received her grandad when he was brought in. She didn't pay attention to any of it. Eventually Ilaria ended up in a tiny office with a counsellor from social services who she could barely bring herself to look at. Ilaria remained silent as she was told that her grandfather's heart had given up.

Ilaria felt numb. It was a state of shock that felt cruel. Like when you wake from a dream and remember the thing you had in that dream is left behind never to be yours again. It didn't make sense that she could be the only one left. Her entire family was gone.

She thought of the dragon and all the lessons she'd been about to learn. It was her twelfth birthday and her grandfather had promised to teach her. Now she was all alone with nothing but questions buzzing around inside her mind.

Finally, Ilaria allowed her attention to drift back to her surroundings inside the hospital. She was sat in the family room opposite a large but friendly looking man called Jack.

'I'm aware that this is going to be a very difficult time for you,' said the calm and soft voice. 'With no other next of kin, we'll need to follow up in a couple of days to make our plans but for now your friend's mother has agreed to take you home with them and look after you for the weekend.'

Jack rifled through some paperwork and looked up at Ilaria again. 'Do you have any questions for me, Ilaria? These can be very confusing times and I just want you to know that I am here to support you.'

Ilaria remained silent for a moment, dreading to ask the question that was playing on her mind the most. She looked up at Jack through her tear-filled eyes and with a fractured voice she asked, 'What is going to happen to me?'

As Ilaria was being led down the corridor to re-join Nawal and Johnny, a nurse came to speak to them.

'You can see him now. If you would like to,' she said.

Everyone turned to Ilaria who looked panicked, not knowing what to do. Of course she wanted to see *him*, but *he* wasn't there anymore. In the room was just his body that would lay still. If she spoke, there would be no reply. If she took his hand it would remain still and cold. She thought of old movies where loved ones lined up at the coffin to say goodbye, not because they wanted to but because it was expected of them. So, Ilaria nodded her head timidly, unable to speak.

'Here, take this.'

The nurse handed Ilaria a plastic bag.

'These were the possessions we found on him. Don't worry, someone will be there to help you sort everything out.'

Ilaria took the bag and followed the nurse into a room where the white sheet in the shape of her grandfather lay before her. The nurse pulled back the sheet and Ilaria shuddered.

'I'll leave you alone for a moment, anything you need, just pop your head outside that door and I'll be there,' said the nurse before leaving the room.

Nawal took Ilaria in her arms and sobbed, 'Ilaria, I'm so sorry, sweetheart. Johnny and I will give you a moment alone. We'll be right outside.'

Nawal left the room, taking Johnny with her. He looked as helpless as a young boy would under such circumstances.

Ilaria stepped closer to her grandfather. She lifted her hand to his head but was too afraid to touch him. Instead she opened the bag to see what was inside. The pendant containing the dragon's heart fragment had dropped to the bottom of the bag along with some random items and, most intriguingly, a rumpled letter that had been sealed. The envelope simply said: Ilaria.

.   .   .

DEAREST HUMMINGBIRD.

So much you do not know about your silly old grandpappy. Just know how much I love you so. And don't feel sad for me, for if you are reading this then I have passed on. But don't see me now as a poor old man who has reached the end of his years. See me for how I lived. You gave me a purpose, even in my old age when your parents were taken from us. Caring for you has been my life's privilege. I was a young boy once, running around the streets with my friends, causing trouble with no direction to be sure of. I was a young man, sent to fight a war that I didn't understand. I lost my first love in that war and thought I would never recover. Then an officer took me in and made me his right hand, he treated me well and I made it through. Years later I was a grown man, with sad stories to tell, but ready to love again. I met your grandmother when we were both older. But we acted like teenagers, riding the amusements at the fairground, pulling candyfloss from each other's hair and talking until the sun came up, oblivious to the time that had passed. Sleeping seemed like such an inconvenient way to spend time when we were together. She never quite settled in Southbourne and we eventually moved back to her hometown of San Casciano. She revealed her secret to me there and I could hardly believe it. But she showed me a world I never knew existed. When your mother was born, she was raised to have a good life. An Italian education is so rich and fulfilling and I know that your mother wanted so much to teach you the things she had learnt as a girl. I'm sorry I couldn't share more with you. I'm just a foolish, timid boy trapped in an old man's body after all. I wish I could have taken you myself to see the delights of the Tuscan hills when you were older. We would have watched the orange sun set across the vineyards and tasted the finest wines in the world. You must go there as soon as you can, for if I am gone, Speranza will need you dearly without a moment to spare. You truly are a remarkable girl.

THAT WAS ALL the letter said. Ilaria didn't know if it had made her feel better or worse. Why did she have to wait until now to learn so much of the man who had raised her? Not once had he spoken to her about her grandmother in such a way. Ilaria flipped over the page, praying for more. But it was blank, he had written as much as he felt he needed to. Ilaria folded the letter up and tucked it into her pocket. She was desperate to ask him questions; so many questions were swimming around her mind and she couldn't stand it. She wondered what came next for her; the world had suddenly become a huge and scary place. Nothing had ever mattered before as her grandfather had been there to take care of her. Now she was to go home with her friend and wait for Jack from social services to tell her where she had to live. She had never been so afraid. The door behind her opened and Johnny's face gawped at her. He was a sweet boy. Without looking back, Ilaria walked straight out of the room, leaving behind the only family she had ever known.

6

Volcanic rock and ash flew into the air from the core of Mount Etna, the Sicilian volcano on the outskirts of the city of Catania. It was the largest eruption since the eighteenth century when the Icelandic volcanic fissure, Lakagigar, had disgorged billions of tons of lava and acid. Half of the livestock on the island had been killed, which led to famine and wiped out a quarter of the Icelandic human population.

The news was breaking on TV as Johnny, Nawal and Ilaria sat and watched, stunned. Apparently, there were several other volcanoes erupting at the same time all over Europe, an event completely unprecedented.

'I can't believe it. What could have caused this?' said Nawal, concerned.

'Mum, do you think those people will be alright? They live right close to the volcano.'

'I hope so, Johnny, I do hope so.'

Johnny became panicked as he thought about his father

stationed in the Andaman Islands. They had visited him one year, shortly after he was stationed there, working as security for a private contractor. It was a tough decision to make and Johnny's father, Benjamin, had made sure to involve both Nawal and Johnny, though Johnny had only been eight at the time. Several of the men and women in the police department in Dorset where Ben had worked were being made redundant so they all agreed that he should take the job offer while it was there.

They had explored Port Blair and other parts of the island on their brief stay, taking a boat ride around the active volcano. Ben had described how it made him feel humble, living with such a powerful natural force as a neighbour.

'Don't worry,' Nawal interrupted Johnny's trail of thought. 'Your father already called to say he is safe, the Barren Island volcano is far off the coast from his office.'

It had been months now since they'd last seen him but he always kept in touch with Nawal and Johnny to let them know he was safe. Every Sunday he called with the same uneventful updates.

'Maybe he will have to come home,' Johnny exclaimed, excited.

'One can dream, darling. One can dream.'

Ilaria sat silently, trying her best to digest the news. It was a welcome distraction and she felt bad for Johnny, worrying as he did. But she couldn't stop wondering if this somehow had something to do with her grandfather. *Had Speranza caused this unbalance?* she wondered, knowing that even Johnny and his mother would think she was mad if she told them her suspicions.

'Ilaria,' Nawal said, with a tone that suggested a change

in subject. 'Would you like me to sit with you in the meeting tomorrow? I'm not sure what they will have to say but if you want me to be there I'm happy to sit beside you.'

Ilaria thought about this. She didn't want the meeting to happen at all.

'Can't I just stay here?'

'I wish that you could, but,' she paused, 'these people know what is best for you, and they are looking for a long-term solution.'

'I wish they would just forget about me, I can go home and take care of myself.'

Smiling, Nawal said, 'And I'm sure that you could, but things don't often work the way we would like them to.'

'I know.' Ilaria stood up from the sofa to head upstairs to Johnny's room where they had set up a camp bed for her. Johnny motioned to follow her but his mother signalled for him to leave Ilaria alone for a while.

Ilaria lay down on her temporary bed, exhausted. She stared up at the ceiling and breathed out a huge sigh as a breeze trickled over her. She hadn't remembered leaving the window open but she enjoyed the refreshing kiss all the same.

After a moment lost in her thoughts, she decided to read her grandfather's letter again. She sat up and pulled the letter out of the bag of possessions that he had left and it was then that she noticed the pendant was missing.

'Oh no,' she said under her breath. She was certain she had put it back in the bag as it was far too important to be lost. She racked her brains about the places she had been where she could have left it but she knew in her heart she had kept it with the letter. Suddenly the open window appeared ominous to her. A dark place that had been soiled while her back was turned. Someone had climbed into the room and stolen the pendant; she knew it as surely as she knew her grandfather was gone.

LATER THAT EVENING, the reports were coming in that there had been twelve volcanic eruptions around Europe. The worst of them were centred around Italy but some eruptions were affecting people even as far as Iceland, and there was no sign of it stopping. It was a match for the eruption that had hit almost two hundred years ago.

Johnny remained transfixed by the television in case the eruptions spread further and there was any news of his father's island. He felt bad as he wanted to take care of Ilaria, but right now, he could think of nothing else.

Nawal was cooking dinner in the kitchen and listening to the radio; the news on every channel was about the volcanoes. A tremendous ash cloud had spread across most of southern Italy and another in Iceland was being blown south by a storm and would soon affect northern Europe. But it was just off the coast of Italy on Oglasa Island where the biggest cloud of all had formed, grounding all nearby air traffic, possibly for weeks to come.

'Ilaria, dinner is ready,' cried out Nawal from the bottom of the stairs. But no answer came. 'Ilaria,' she shouted again, louder but still without response.

'Johnny, turn that television off and go and check on Ilaria, let her know that dinner is ready please.'

'Yes, Mum,' Johnny said as he switched off the television and ran upstairs into his room. When he creaked the door open, to his surprise, he found the window wide open and some of Ilaria's things were missing, as was she. He found a note left on the bedside table that she had weighed down with one of his toy dinosaurs. Johnny ran straight to the kitchen clutching the note and stared at Nawal, panicked.

'Oh no,' Nawal sighed as she saw the note. 'Well, read it to me then.'

So Johnny did, in a sombre voice.

'Johnny, I hope you and Nawal will forgive me for leaving unannounced, but I have something to do that is very important and I can't waste time being carted around by social services. I am worried that something very bad could be happening and I need to know if it has something to do with my family. Stay safe, Ilaria.'

Nawal and Johnny shared a look of confusion, and it dawned on them both in that moment that they didn't know anything about her family at all.

THE PORT WAS in a state of frenzy. Queues to the ticket office were spilling out onto the streets and blocking the roads that led to Plymouth harbour. Holidaymakers and business men and women were all shouting and scrambling across each other trying to reach the ferry that was soon to depart.

Ilaria, who awoke aching from her overnight coach journey, strained her eyes to see the chaos ahead through the window. She realised that she wasn't going anywhere fast if she stayed seated on the coach, so she got up, gathered her things and made her way to the front where the driver was slumped over his wheel, frustrated and bored.

'Excuse me, sir,' Ilaria said. 'Can I get off here, please? I'm late meeting my family.'

The driver hit a button without saying a word and waved her off, and soon a flurry of other passengers on the coach followed her lead.

Ilaria ran through the crowds, clutching her bag tightly, apologising to everyone as she knocked into them on her way to the ticket office.

'Excuse me, young girl, there is a line here for tickets, thank you very much,' shouted a stern middle-aged man in a suit.

'Oh yes, I am sorry, but my family is already boarding you see.'

'Then you're in the wrong place, this is the line for buying tickets, we won't be getting on a ferry for days. You'd better go and speak to that man over there.' The stern man suddenly became a lot friendlier and shouted out to the port worker to get his attention.

'No! It's alright, I can find them on my own,' Ilaria suddenly panicked, not really knowing what she was doing, but she certainly didn't want any unwelcome attention.

The man didn't pay any notice however and replied, 'Don't worry, he'll get you through to the ferry.'

The port worker approached the fence that was crowded with people. He craned his head over the throng to improve his chances of hearing what the fuss was about.

'I say, over here, this young girl has been separated from her family. They are boarding the next ferry.'

The port worker looked about anxiously. 'Right, well. You'd better come through to me then. Come on push through.' He cupped his mouth in his hands to make his voice travel further. 'Ladies and gentlemen, please make way for the girl, she's lost her family.'

Ilaria's cheeks flushed scarlet but she pushed through the crowd of people all the same. She turned and gave a wave to the smiling businessman who seemed very happy with himself for doing such a good deed. But Ilaria felt anything but safe now; her plan, not that she really had one, was about to fall apart around her. She would be sent back to Southbourne and collected by the authorities in no time.

'So, where are you headed, young lady?' the port worker asked as he walked her through the workers' pathway towards the ferry.

'Erm, well, Italy,' Ilaria said, not knowing where this particular ferry was headed at all. She had intended to buy a ticket and figure out a route but amidst all this uproar, that idea had gone by the wayside.

'Italy, ay? You do realise this ferry is headed to Santander, don't you?'

'Er, yes of course. I meant that eventually I... I mean *we* will arrive in Italy. By way of Santander of course.'

'Strange route you've picked. I suppose it can't be helped, what with all air traffic being grounded. Well, here we are then. Can you see them anywhere?'

Ilaria pretended to look for her family and shook her head.

'Oh dear, well. Do you have your documentation with you?' asked the port worker.

'No, you see, my father has it with him,' Ilaria lied.

'You mean he boarded the ferry carrying your documents without you?'

Suddenly a burly woman in a very tight fitting uniform interrupted them. She had a worried look on her face.

'What's all this fuss then? This girl shouldn't be on this side of the fence, Max, you know that.'

'Yes, sorry, ma'am, but she lost her family. They boarded without her and I think her father forgot he had all her paperwork with him.'

His manager's expression changed instantly.

'Oh, good you made it! Max dear, hurry up and get this young lady on board. Her family were expecting her to arrive with her auntie tomorrow.'

The burly woman turned to Ilaria and put her hand on her shoulder.

'You must have been lucky on the roads,' she said.

'Yes, we were!' Ilaria agreed.

'What's your name?' asked Max.

'It's, er, Ilaria.'

'Erilliaria? What a peculiar nickname,' the burly woman chortled.

Ilaria was not best pleased with that comment but now was not the time to argue.

The woman continued, 'It doesn't sound at all like Elizabeth.'

Ilaria panicked, she had given herself away. The stocky woman frowned at her for a moment and then her smile widened.

'Well, I don't understand kids nowadays, must be all those fantasy stories you read.'

Ilaria nodded in agreement. 'Yes, that's right.'

'Eriilia... er... Elizabeth here will need assistance on board looking for her family, Max. Parsons is their name. Be a dear and make sure that one of the deck crew helps her will you.'

'Yes, of course,' he replied.

Ilaria thought how idiotic this pair were and was a little hurt that they thought her real name was a silly nickname, but she was also very thankful for it. So, Max led the fake Elizabeth Parsons onto the ferry and she abruptly bid him farewell before he had time to realise he'd forgotten all about helping her to find her family on board.

A large horn sounded as the ferry began to pull away from the port and Ilaria ran up the stairs and through the hallway, seeing hundreds of passengers lying on the floor, ready for a long and uncomfortable journey. Extra tickets had been sold to alleviate some of the demand caused by the grounded flights and, as luck would have it, Ilaria could easily get lost amongst the crowds.

She ran out onto the deck at the back of the ferry and a strong breeze caused her to shudder, but she ignored the chill as she saw the coast of Britain disappearing into the distance. It was the first time she had left the island since she was a baby. Now she was a stowaway on her way to Italy by way of Santander, wherever that was. She was sure she had no idea.

7

Santander wasn't at all what Ilaria expected. After twenty hours lying on the floor of a smelly, noisy ferry she had hoped to land somewhere exotic. Instead she was met by a grey, wet and windy port town, not so unlike the one she had left. The main difference was that there were statues and large buildings spread out amongst the concourse where the coast was met by large open spaces and wide roads.

Ilaria wandered up and down the footpath trying to find something that resembled a map but she couldn't find anything useful at all. She was becoming quite sleepy as a voice inside her head told her.

You'd better find out where you are, girl.

Ilaria thought it was strange that she was referring to herself in her mind in the third person. Maybe she had invented a surrogate for her grandfather to keep her company.

'North coast of Spain of course,' said a young man, with a cigarette sticking out of his mouth. It turned out Ilaria was thinking out loud and she would have been embarrassed were it not for the intrusion of a cloud of smoke that hit her in the face. She waved her hand about frantically trying not to breathe it in. The stranger chuckled at her before helping waft it away.

'Sorry about that, can't help where the wind blows,' he said.

Some hours had passed since Ilaria had begun circling the port on foot and as it was almost night time now, she decided to find the courage to speak to the stranger.

'Do you have a map of the world by any chance?' she asked.

The man laughed and as he went to take another puff of his cigarette he gestured to his girlfriend who was sat next to him.

The young woman smiled. 'Come and take a seat... What was your name?' she asked.

'It's Ilaria.'

'Right, well, Ilaria. Come and see here.' The young woman pulled out a traveller's guide from her backpack and opened out the inlay map on the stony steps of Santander Cathedral where Ilaria now sat beside her.

'We are here. At the most northern tip of Spain,' said the young woman, pointing to the map, 'and where is it you are headed?'

Ilaria hesitated for a second, feeling stupid and completely lost. 'I'm going to Italy, to a town where my family are from.'

'Right, well that isn't on this map, I'm afraid. This only shows most of Spain, Portugal and some of the southern border of France. Who are you with if you don't mind me asking?'

'It's just me now,' Ilaria replied.

'Oh.' The young woman was lost for words and for a moment seemed as though she was about to question Ilaria further, but decided against it. The young man finally stamped out his cigarette and turned to face Ilaria.

'Listen, we're catching a bus in the morning to Seville, it's in Andalusia nearer the south. You might be able to head to the south coast from there and make your way to Sicily by sea.'

'Frank! Don't be ridiculous, that's far too long winded. She'd be better off going by land across France.'

'Look, all I am saying is, we have a spare ticket.' Frank turned to Ilaria. 'My friend is stuck in Glasgow, thanks to all the flights being grounded and you are welcome to use it. Have you seen the bus station? There are people queuing around the block and there is nothing for days. You're welcome to join them but I think you'll end up sleeping on the street outside the station for a week!'

'I suppose we can help you get to Malaga at least,' said the young woman. 'I'm going to Seville to study flamenco. It's the most famous part of the world for flamenco you know?'

Ilaria shook her head. 'What is flamenco?' she asked.

'Oh dear, well that settles it. You absolutely must come to Seville and see it for yourself. I'm Antonia, nice to meet you, Ilaria.'

Antonia held out her hand to Ilaria and they shook hands.

'Pleased to meet you, Antonia, and Frank,' Ilaria said,

looking from one to the other. Frank nodded his head in a casual but approving manner.

Antonia stood up and wiped a thin layer of dust off the top of her thighs. 'That's strange, well, we'd better get to our hostel, it's a long journey in the morning.'

'Where are you staying, Ilaria?' asked Frank as he threw his rucksack on his back.

'Oh, I hadn't really figured that bit out yet.'

'Of course not,' he sighed.

THE CONVERSATION at the hostel didn't go as well as Frank had hoped. Without any ID or payment, Ilaria had been refused entry and despite the complaints of Antonia and Frank, the night porter was having none of it. Ilaria had told them not to worry and that she would meet them at the bus station the following morning. Antonia was afraid to leave Ilaria alone at night but before she could insist on staying with her, Ilaria had picked up her things and set off into the night to explore Santander one last time. Fortunately, it was not too cold and with her limited supplies, Ilaria managed to get fairly comfortable on the base of a statue where she rested her head, and through sheer exhaustion, managed to fall asleep.

That night she dreamed about her grandfather. She heard his wonderful laugh and saw his cheeky grin bearing down on her from the platform where he stood. They were drifting together on a sailboat towards the horizon and Brian was steering them towards a setting sun. Ilaria felt free and safe, watching as the waves lapped against the side of the boat.

She closed her eyes and felt the warm breeze against her

face, listening as the fabric of the sails billowed in the wind. It was the most welcome moment of peace. But suddenly she heard a roaring sound, it was the sound of a dragon screaming from afar. Ilaria opened her eyes and the roaring sound of the dragon became the thunderous clap of a storm and then she realised she was alone on the boat and the steering wheel was spinning uncontrollably. Flashes of light tore through the sky and a bolt of lightning struck so close that it almost hit the deck. Ilaria, with no other plan in mind, ran towards the wheel and tried with all her might to stop it spinning, but instead the force of the ferocious wheel threw her to her side and she slid across the deck, just as a large wave landed on top of her and she spluttered, gasping for air as the salty water ran down her face.

'Stop it! Please, stop!' Ilaria screamed as she jumped to her feet, her face soaking wet and there she stood staring at Frank who was in hysterics, having just thrown a bottle of water over her face. Antonia slapped him on the shoulder, clearly disapproving of his prank.

'What? Everyone knows it's the best way to wake someone up when they're dreaming,' he said. 'Don't they?'

'You're cruel, Frank Thomas, very cruel,' said Antonia as she helped Ilaria compose herself by gathering her things. Ilaria was not quite sure if she felt in shock from the rude awakening or from the brief glimpse she had had of her grandfather and the moment of joy she had felt before it was shattered by the storm.

Keeping her thoughts to herself, Ilaria followed Antonia and Frank as the three wandered off together towards the bus station and boarded the coach to Seville.

The journey was long and winding, and the heat became

almost unbearable as they neared the south of Spain. It didn't help that the air conditioning in the bus was broken, though according to the elderly woman in the seat next to her, this was normal. She was a regular on this route and was currently on her way to visit her grandson. She was concerned about Ilaria travelling alone at such a young age but Ilaria had explained that Antonia was her big sister and was taking care of her.

The lady complained about the volcanic ash that was spreading. Her husband was supposed to be returning from a meeting in London so they could visit their grandson together but he had been stuck there.

Ilaria nodded in agreement and smiled politely as her neighbour nattered on about how wonderful her grandson was in her broken English.

He was a keen musician, who often played at tapas bars around the town centre to help pay his tuition fees. The more Ilaria heard about Seville, the more she felt like it truly must be a magical place. The Giralda Tower of the cathedral, the Alcazar palace and flamenco bars of Triana were just a few of the places she had been told she must go and see. Ilaria couldn't help but feel enraptured by this magical place but also thought how far she still had to go to get to Tuscany.

Her mind wandered and she stared out of the window, fear and panic taking hold of her as she suddenly realised how far she was from home. Nawal and Johnny must be so worried about her and although she had considered trying to phone them to explain, she knew that the moment she heard their voices she would be too weak to ignore their pleading for her to return home to Southbourne.

Ilaria was entranced by the spinning wheels of a car driving parallel to them. They span so fast that they appeared to be moving backwards. She thought to herself that maybe life was like that—if you tried to go forwards too fast you'd lose control and end up going backwards. Perhaps her journey was hopeless and, though she had no idea what she was supposed to do if she ever did make it to San Casciano, she clung onto the few stories of her mother and grandmother that she could recall.

The advice from her grandfather played over and over in her mind. She was determined to go there and find someone who had known them. After all, it was a very small town where her family had come from she had been told. *There must be someone there who knew them,* she thought.

Ilaria pulled out the letter from her grandfather and began to read it once more, thinking about the pendant that had gone missing with the dragon's heart fragment. She felt anxious about being away from home, though more anxious still about the journey ahead of her. She tried to focus on the task at hand as the enormity of the journey to Italy overwhelmed her. She folded up the letter and stared through the window at the landscape whipping past her before slipping into a deep sleep. The coach rocked her back and forth like a baby in a cradle and she clutched herself tight, hoping to see her mother in her dreams.

8

A pack of wolves must work together for a hunt to be successful. They stalk their target for days until they are certain the terrain and weather is suited to their favour, for fear of their prey escaping. Snowy weather conditions suit them best, as often they rely on the animals they chase being slowed by the thickness and the cold. It was this principle that allowed the heart thieves to hunt the dragons, as the underground environment was claustrophobic for them and difficult to navigate.

The creatures would often stalk the dragons into the deepest, narrowest passages before striking. Their victim's wings restricted by the cavern walls making it near impossible for a dragon to turn its head to face an attack coming from behind. It was said that the elongated lifespan dragons enjoyed from their second heart, was the foremost reason the heart thieves hunted them. The order of people who were bonded with the dragons, known as Tamers, would scout the tunnels looking for any sign of ambush and communicate with them through thought. It was exhausting for a human to telepathize with a dragon, so they would take caution to send warning at the right moment. But it had been many years since an attack on a dragon had taken place.

Speranza had grown wild since Brian had died. He grasped for some sign of Ilaria in his mind but found himself forgetting why she was important. He didn't quite understand what had been the purpose of the bond he had harboured for centuries. All he knew now was that his rage was growing and to satisfy his wildness he was breathing more ferocious flames beneath the earth's surface than he had for a thousand years.

Speranza was growing stronger and fiercer by the day. His human connection had been severed and his true dragon instincts were coming to the surface. He felt more alive now. The outbursts of rage that he suffered had seen him enter into a kind of dance, relinquishing his energy to the centre of the earth and when his flames heated the molten rocks of the core it too grew in power, raising its temperature to an unbalanced level and causing devastation above the surface in the guise of unprecedented volcanic eruptions.

The other dragons tried to reason with Speranza, repeating the concerns and fears of their own human counterparts, but they no longer made sense to him. So, he continued his ballet of fire and energy, with no sign of the tragic opera coming to an end.

A LOUD AND distinct tapping sound rang throughout the room as the heels of the dancer's shoes rapped the ground.

Her red dress swirled from side to side, reflecting a warm glow across the ceiling like a pulsating fire.

Ilaria was stunned by the cold, serious expressions of the dancer and guitarist who accompanied her. Their gazes were matched by the crowd, who sat in silence admiring the performance. Beside Ilaria sat Antonia and Frank, who were both mesmerised and clapped heartily along with the locals at the appropriate moments. It almost seemed like part of the show, the way that the audience participated between movements of the music and dance. Ilaria felt heartened by what she saw. It was truly magical; somehow every person in the bar was connected by a commonality that transcended race or culture. But Ilaria also feared that she was being distracted and wasn't sure how to say goodbye to the young couple who had brought her here. If she told them she was leaving, they may try to convince her to stay a little longer, so Ilaria excused herself to go to the bathroom and, clutching her bag, she walked out into the streets of Triana, on the western bank of the Seville canal.

She made her way back to the centre of town, across the San Telmo bridge and headed for the centuries-old cathedral where the coach had dropped them off earlier that day. It was around ten o'clock in the evening and the streets were bustling with parties. Outside every bar was a myriad of tables, filled with people enjoying their evening meals. Fires burned in the side streets where the Sevillians sat and sang together.

Ilaria's head was spinning as the streets of Seville were like a labyrinth. She kept looking up at the skies for any sign of the Giralda Tower to mark her way but it was nowhere to be seen. She headed down a narrow alleyway that was derelict save for a shadowy figure walking towards her.

The figure was holding the leash of a large dog and before Ilaria knew what was happening, the animal had broken free from its owner and was running towards her barking at the top of its voice. Ilaria froze, praying that it would stop but as it came closer, stepping into the light of a street lamp, she saw its teeth bearing down on her.

Ilaria turned and ran towards a small passage between two buildings and prayed for an open doorway that she could escape through. But there was none. She spun her head back towards the dog and as she did so she tripped over a large object in the alley.

Ilaria came crashing to the ground but as she braced herself to crack her head on the tiled stone floor, a soft shape cushioned her fall and she was uninjured. The dog was barking at her and she felt vulnerable, a young girl who was lost in a strange place. She closed her eyes tight, imagining in the next moment that she would be eaten alive. But she wasn't.

'Parada, Amic, déjala en paz!!' shouted the man as he ran towards his dog who was now whining, and seemed to be concerned about Ilaria. It began to lick Ilaria's leg, which had been grazed as she had fallen.

'Lo siento, lo siento mucho!' said the man, pleading for forgiveness.

'I'm sorry. I don't understand Spanish,' Ilaria replied.

The man held out his hand to help her up from the ground and Ilaria then realised that she had tumbled into a stack of rubbish bags at the back entrance to a restaurant.

She began wiping the dirt off her jeans, then she noticed the hole by her knee that was bleeding.

'Fantastic,' she said to herself sarcastically.

'I am so, so sorry, miss. Amic is wild but he never means to harm nothing.'

'It's okay,' Ilaria lied. 'Amic, that's a nice name, what does it mean?'

'Ah, Amico. It means friend.'

Ilaria's ears perked up. 'Of course, it's Italian. I should have recognised it,'

'Dai, parli Italiano?'

'No sorry, not really, I just know a few words. Are you from Italy?'

'Si, si! Sono da Siena. Sorry, I mean, I am from Siena. You know it? A beautiful Tuscan town, close to Firenze.'

Ilaria smiled at the man and reached down to pat Amic, who was wining at her, on the head. 'Siena is not too far from where my family is from, I think. You speak English perfectly. I'm sorry, what was your name?'

'Dai, my English is a little crazy, no? My name is Dario. I learn English here in Seville. Strange I know because 'iz a Spanish town, but most of the jobs here are impossible to get if you don't speak the English and Spanish so I studied at a school nearby for almost two years. And you? Where are you from? What do I call you?'

'Ilaria. I am from the south of England, but my family is from Italy originally. I am trying to get there.'

'You are a long way from Tuscany, Ilaria, and if you don't mind me saying, it's a little dangerous to travel alone, a distance such as this. Especially for one so young.'

'I'm used to being alone.' Ilaria said the words and they

pricked her heart, but the strangest thing was that they clearly pricked Dario too.

'No one gets used to being alone, we just somehow keep on moving.'

The man seemed concerned as he said the words. Ilaria looked at him and suddenly her excitement at meeting Dario dwindled as she realised that what he said must be true. She was miles away from her destination and had no idea how she was going to get there with no one to help her.

'I guess I'd better keep moving then...' Ilaria couldn't think of anything else to say.

'Allora, Ilaria, I might have a solution to part of your problem. A friend of mine is sailing to Sicily tomorrow. I'm sure if you offered to help on her boat she would take you as her passenger.'

'Really? Do you think so?' Ilaria's eyes lit up with hope.

'Yes, I can call to her right away, but listen there is a problem. She is preparing her voyage already, in Malaga. I don't know how we get you there in time.'

'Oh, I see,' Ilaria said, also not knowing how to get to Malaga by tomorrow morning.

'Wait! Come with me, I think I know someone who can help us.' Dario suddenly seemed optimistic and he ran off down the street with his dog Amic, and Ilaria, with no other option available, ran after him across a plaza that was lined with dozens of orange trees and then around a corner towards a loud bar that was packed with people drinking and shouting.

Dario and Ilaria went inside and pushed their way through the crowds. It was a very dingy place and it seemed to Ilaria that growing a foot-long beard or wearing scruffy clothes must be an entry requirement; judging by all the clientele. Ilaria could barely hear anything other than the ensemble of voices and music blasting from the speakers but she watched as Dario pushed his way to the bar and leant over to shout in the ear of a very drunk man who was being propped up by the counter. The drunk turned to look at Ilaria and nodded his head in approval before shaking hands with Dario and going back to his drink.

Dario walked over towards Ilaria and shouted in her ear, 'This guy, he is a friend of mine, a photographer. He is leaving tomorrow with a group of people who are going to stay in Morocco to photograph the Atlas Mountains. They were supposed to fly, but as you know, it is impossible now with the ash cloud spread across the skies, so instead they will go by sea. There is one space in the bus, leaving at seven am in the morning. It is dropping them in Gibraltar but you are in luck because they need to pick up a friend in Malaga first, so you will swap places with that girl there and meet my friend, Silvia, who sets off in the evening.' Dario clasped his hands together joyously as he laid out the plans. Ilaria's head was spinning. Too much information.

'You seem to know everyone, everywhere,' Ilaria said, smiling.

'Of course, I am a tour guide, I must know everyone and everything. Now, all you need to do is pay me twenty thousand pesetas to complete the arrangement.'

Ilaria was silent. She barely had enough money to buy a loaf of bread. Her heart sank as she realised that she was completely stuck and just as she was about to admit she had hardly any money, Dario burst out laughing.

'You British, you make me laugh. Sometimes you have no wit at all. I am joking of course, Ilaria, there is no fee.'

'Sorry, this is all a bit new to me. If something sounds too good to be true, it probably is.' Ilaria recalled her grandfather's words proudly.

'When fortune smiles upon us, we must grab hold of her and never let go. Goodbye, Ilaria. Raul will take care of you, and please say hello to Silvia for me, she is a feisty one and once broke my heart but she will take good care of you. Good luck!'

Dario ruffled her hair with his hand and led Amic out of the bar as Ilaria watched him go. She suddenly felt very strange and alone again. It was as if she had been swept along by a whirlwind and then cast aside again before she knew what was happening.

Ilaria was afraid and didn't trust Raul. He looked scary and she hated scary drunk men. She wanted so desperately to run but her jelly legs stayed attached to the floor of the bar.

Too late to change my mind now, she thought as she timidly shuffled to the corner and found a small table to sleep at, staying out of the way but keeping an eye on Raul, afraid that in his drunken state he would forget all about her and his promise to take her to Malaga in the morning.

The night passed slowly and as other photographers started to arrive in the bar as the sun came up, Ilaria relaxed with relief that everything was going to be okay.

THE JOURNEY the next day was long, but the scenery was beautiful. Ilaria sat in the back seat next to Raul who slept the entire journey, clearly having drunk too much the night before. The rest of the photographers chatted the entire way and Ilaria couldn't understand a word, so she continued to stare out of the window, enjoying the ride and admiring the Andalusian scenery.

She wondered what it would be like to sail across the ocean in a small boat. She knew that it wouldn't be the same as boarding a ferry but she certainly couldn't have envisaged the hard work and dangers of the ocean that awaited her.

9

A large bump and crashing sound threw Ilaria forwards and disturbed her rest. A horrible metallic sound of metal grinding against rock penetrated her ears like nails on a chalk board. Ilaria felt her stomach lurch as the bus tilted forwards over the edge of a mountainous pathway. The passengers screamed as the driver tried to reverse back onto the road but the rear wheels were elevated in the air and no contact could be made. The wheels span uncontrollably as the engine revved harder and harder.

Ilaria could see a huge drop to their side through her window as the bus swayed back and forth as the passengers rose from their seats shouting words she could not understand.

At the back of the bus she saw one of the photographers smashing the back window with a drink canteen, creating a hole big enough to climb through. But as the he began to climb through it the other passengers shouted at him to stop.

'Espera, espera!' cried Raul from beside Ilaria. 'We can't lose any weight or the bus will topple forwards off the cliff.'

Ilaria saw Raul waving frantically at the entire bus.

'We need to get the wheels back on the ground! Please stay calm.'

Nervousness was evident in his voice and he was no longer in any kind of drunken state.

While Raul tried to reason with the others, another one of the photographers ran to the front of the bus and demanded that the driver open the side door so they could jump out. But their weight unbalanced the bus and it slipped further down the gravel edge towards the shear drop beneath them.

'Nobody move!' screamed Raul. This time his voice was enraged and the chaotic distress of the passengers was silenced.

'The only thing keeping us alive is our combined weight, the moment that any of us exits the bus the weight of the vehicle will send us over the edge. We need to stay calm and think of a solution before we act.'

Raul was right and they all knew it. The survival instinct of the individual passengers was a chorus and they must sing together as a unit or none of them would be heard again.

'We need help from someone outside of the bus, but it's still early and we may not see a passing car for hours. Why did we take this stupid road, it's barely safe for a bicycle!' said the photographer who had broken the rear window.

The driver perked up at this and switched on his loudspeaker. 'Excuse me! This road is the best way to get to Malaga due to all the closures and road blocks and I didn't hear any objections until that damn boulder in the road came out of nowhere.'

The bickering began again and Raul hung his head. They were getting nowhere and fast. He looked at Ilaria and she sensed his eyes moving up and down as though he were weighing her up. He was.

'You're the smallest of us, Ilaria, we can probably afford to lose you, but you must find help. Maybe if you climb out of that window you can head up the hill and see across the valley? I think it's our only chance,' said Raul.

Ilaria gulped. *Wasn't this escapade hard enough already?* Now it was down to her to save a bus full of photographers. She just wanted to escape and run away as fast as she dared. But she knew she couldn't.

'It's okay, we'll be fine,' Raul continued. 'Chicos, vamos a la parte de atrás del autobús. If we weigh down the back together while Ilaria goes to find help we shouldn't slip further down the cliff.'

Fortunately, the full bus agreed to the plan as in this instance a unanimous decision was essential. Ilaria felt all eyes on her as she made her way to the back window and as she clambered through it she saw a large boulder that was stuck beneath the wheel arch. If the rock moved or broke, the bus would slip and nothing would stop it careering down the slope. She felt the pressure from the gazes of the dozen passengers glaring at her, relying on her to save them. A twelve-year-old girl, away from home for the first time, was their only hope.

'Vay, chica, don't let us down, just tell the first person you find!' was the last thing Raul shouted before Ilaria ran across the road and started to clamber up the rocky hill to reach the vantage point above.

The early morning sun was piercing through a thin patch of the ash-filled sky and it made the climb hot work. Ilaria was sweating and coughing with all the dust that had been kicked up around her. A fragile breeze had opened up a patch of clear sky but it also loosened the dry earth and as she wiped her brow with her sleeve she could see the dirt she had smeared from her face.

She neared the top, grappling some thin weeds to hoist her to her vantage point. She looked back down and amidst the beautiful Andalusian vista, she saw the lonely bus, precariously balancing on the edge of the cliff. On the edge of life and death. She turned to look across the valley at the other side but there was nothing other than deadly silent roads at the bottom. A small gathering of derelict houses was all she could see in the distance. She squinted to sharpen her vision and saw some hanging clothes, drying on one of the rooftops. She figured if the clothes had just been hung this morning then there could be someone there who could help them.

Ilaria ran down the other side of the valley from where she had come, furthering the distance between her and the busload of photographers. She slipped and skidded on the loose soil but maintained her footing and when she reached the road she began to run towards the gathering of buildings. She wheezed and sweated more, as dehydration set in. But in the distance she saw a mirage-like image of a sandstorm rushing towards her. At its centre was a large truck and Ilaria began to jump up and down, waving her arms around like a crazed person.

Before long, the truck neared her position, but it did not slow and Ilaria had to move to the side of the road as the truck careened past, covering her head to toe in dust and debris from the road.

Ilaria couldn't cope anymore and she fell to her knees on the grass verge beside the valley pass, curling up in a ball. She was dizzy and thirsty and her vision blurred, as she felt a nausea in the pit of her stomach and closed her eyes.

'Ciao, ragazza! Hello, girl, wake up! Wake up!' sounded an unfamiliar voice. 'Are you alright? What are you doing?'

Ilaria rolled onto her side and saw the face of a very concerned woman.

'I-I'm sorry! I just wanted to save them,' Ilaria said feebly.

'What are you talking about? How long have you been lying there? You are lucky I didn't run you over with my van!'

Ilaria looked beside the woman and saw a small pickup truck, it was loaded with some form of engine and ropes and… 'Sails! You're a sailor?' Ilaria blurted out.

'Yes, that's right. And you're her, aren't you? The girl who wants to get to Italy? I knew it, somehow when I first laid my eyes on you, that you must be the girl Dario had called me about, but, what are you doing here?' she asked.

'Our bus got stuck on a mountain path, they're all in trouble. I came to find help.'

It was a miracle that destiny would bring them together like this, but as someone who lived by the fate of the seas, Silvia rushed to the driver's seat and started the engine.

'Ilaria, I believe help is exactly what you have found. Take me to them at once.'

.   .   .

SILVIA HAD TURNED out to be exactly as Ilaria had
expected. She felt like she had known her for her whole life
at the first sound of her voice. She explained what had
happened and Silvia couldn't believe how lucky they were
that she had been collecting supplies from her family estate
in the valley where she had driven past Ilaria just moments
earlier. Ilaria directed her to the bus where they had crashed
into the rock, wishing she hadn't experienced such a
traumatic episode, but wondering whether it hadn't
somehow guided Silvia to her. It was almost like her journey
was a fabled story and every part of it so far was a part of her
destiny.

They pulled up alongside the bus and Silvia tied some of
her sailing rope to the back trailer clamp. She used the winch
that was attached to her van to make the rope tight and then
one by one the photographers jumped out of the bus.

Once the driver, who was the last to leave, had thrown
the final piece of luggage down and jumped out of the back
window, they attempted to pull the bus back up but the
gears grinded and Silvia's van began to edge closer to the
edge of the cliff.

Silvia pulled out a multitool and sawed at the rope,
severing it and sending the bus plummeting to the depths of
the cavern below. It crumpled like a paper mâché house that
a younger Ilaria had once made for her action figures, before
playing the part of the giant and trampling all over it.

She remembered the overwhelming feeling of power and
superiority that the game had brought her as well as the look

on her grandfather's face as she destroyed what she had built, and the guilt that had rattled her afterwards.

Ilaria considered how fragile they all were, stuck on that bus and how easily they could have all been killed in an instant. She thought of Speranza and wondered if a dragon regarded people as dispensable. Just as she had treated her toy paper house that day.

10

'Hoist the sails,' Silvia cried, as Ilaria did her best to pull the lines that would allow the yacht to catch the wind and set them on their way.

Silvia hadn't said much more to Ilaria since the accident. Time had been short and an easterly wind was forecast to blow down the Mediterranean Sea that threatened to slow their progress to the port in Sicily. Ilaria had been given a set of instructions that made little sense to her and needed them all repeated at least twice.

'Ilaria, to port side and check the rigging, I think we have too much slack.' Silvia shouted out as she steered them at a slight angle to catch the airstream. Ilaria ran and checked the knots, which all seemed fine to her so she turned and gave a thumbs up to Silvia who set the wheel in position and finally relaxed into the journey.

'Well, that should do us for the next hour or so, but with this wind due to come against us we'll have to zigzag all the way to Palermo, which is going to be very slow.' Silvia gazed out across the sea as she analysed their voyage and Ilaria went to sit near her at the bow of the sailboat.

'I never realised that sailing could be so confusing,' Ilaria admitted as she shuffled onto the wooden crate beside Silvia, who laughed.

'Yes, it certainly can be. It becomes trickier when you don't have the wind on your side, but we'll make do as it's still blowing from the west at the moment.'

'How long have you been sailing for?' Ilaria asked.

'Well, I guess about ten years now. My family come from a background of pearl divers off the coast of Gibraltar. Not many pearls left now though, so I spend the summer months transporting goods between Spain and Italy.'

'It seems like a lot of work for one person.'

'Yes it is. Normally I have a small crew with me but everyone got stuck in Malta after their flights were cancelled. Fortunately, I have you to help me now,' Silvia said, smiling at Ilaria. 'How old are you, Ilaria?'

'I'm twelve.'

'Oh, I thought you were older.'

'I feel like I've aged a few years this past week alone.' Ilaria sighed deeply thinking of the journey that had brought her here so far.

'Yes, Dario told me a bit about your other adventures, before you nearly got driven off a cliff. I don't suppose many twelve-year-old girls can claim to have had the escapades that you have.'

'I guess not,' Ilaria said with her heart sinking, wondering whether she would have been better off in the care of social services back in Southbourne. That was someone else's life.

Silvia gestured to Ilaria and pointed to the south.

'You see that, to the starboard side. That's the north coast of Africa. I see it all the time from this shipping lane. But I've never once been there.'

'Really? Why don't you go?'

'I don't know, I always mean to but then I get busy with life, I guess. Our friend Dario is partly to blame for that.'

'Oh, what did he do?'

'Cosa non ha fatto lui... Ahi. Well we were engaged for a long time. He used to work on the boat with me but he never liked being at sea so he moved to Seville to start his tour company. We kind of drifted apart after that.'

'I'm sorry to hear that,' Ilaria said sympathetically. 'Does it ever get any easier?'

'Does what get easier?'

'Life?' Ilaria asked, pleadingly.

Silvia shook her head before finding the words to respond. 'No, it's always this way.'

Silvia stood and went to adjust the course of the sailboat. She licked her forefinger and held it up in the air.

'The wind is still blowing in our favour. We should make the most of this before it changes direction.'

'How can you tell just with your finger?' Ilaria asked, fascinated.

'Well, if you lick your finger, the wind will cause you to feel a cold sensation, so by holding it in the air you know which direction the wind is coming from depending on which part of your finger feels the coldest.'

'You know a lot of interesting things.'

'I never was one for an office job.' Silvia winked at Ilaria and set them at a direct trajectory towards Sicily.

Hours passed by peacefully and the sun began to set, casting rich purple hues across the stern of the sailboat where Ilaria had curled up in a ball, wrapped in a blanket. It was a beautiful Moroccan woollen cover that Dario had bought for Silvia on a trip he made to Tangier. It was incredibly comfortable and warm and it made her feel safe.

A couple of days passed with the same routine. The winds had changed direction and they were now sailing against them. It had slowed them down but they were still making reasonable progress.

Sailing, Ilaria realised, gave you plenty of time to reflect. Something about the simplicity of it. The endless surrounding ocean somehow simplified the task at hand. Her worries seemed to lessen as she could do nothing about any of them; for now, she was heading for Palermo and that was all she needed to consider.

As another evening sun rested on the horizon, Ilaria spotted splashes in the water. It was a family of dolphins jumping in and out of the sea, causing ripples to reflect the light of the increasingly reddening sky.

'Dolphins,' Ilaria cried out, 'They're wonderful, Silvia!'

'Yes, you often see them around this area. We're near the border of Algeria and Tunisia. They enjoy the beauty of the sun setting as much as we do. Dolphins are one of the most beautiful, kind and intelligent creatures in the world.'

'Is that why we have theme parks where you can go to see them?'

'Yes, I am afraid so, it is one of the horrible things us humans do. We see something beautiful and then we take control of it and turn it into a business. No matter what suffering is caused. If it were up to me I would free all the animals in the world.'

Ilaria went quiet suddenly, thinking about her family and the dragons. They too were magnificent animals, surely they belonged in the sky and not underground. Ilaria imagined how painful and restrictive it must be to live in those tunnels. She thought about the dream when she had seen the dragon, and wondered if it were a truthful depiction.

'Are you okay, Ilaria? You seem worried about something.'

'Oh, it's nothing. I was just daydreaming.'

'Are you sure? You could capsize the boat with the weight on your shoulders.' Silvia looked past Ilaria then and her expression changed. She ran quickly to the side of the boat, panicking. 'Oh no!'

Ilaria ran to her side to see what had happened. It was there they saw a baby dolphin flapping about uncontrollably, a plastic bag wrapped around its snout. The dolphin's family circled it, helpless.

'We have to help it,' Silvia said, as she began to tie a safety cord to her floatation device. 'Ilaria, I need you to keep control of this line. You'll have to help me back to the boat when I'm finished.'

'What are you going to do?' Ilaria asked, as she held onto the safety cord.

Silvia climbed up onto the side of the boat closest to the dolphin and readied herself to jump into the ocean. 'Don't worry, just keep hold of the line.'

Silvia dived in, floating instantly to the surface. She swam towards the dolphin and tried to calm it down so she could unwrap the plastic bag. The dolphin continued to flail about but Silvia managed to peel away the bag and she tucked it underneath a strap on her outfit.

The dolphin swam back to its family and after a moment of relief, made a beautiful sound, calling out towards Silvia. Ilaria liked to think that it was saying thank you. Silvia plunged her hands deep into the water around her and looked furious.

'Ilaria, pull me back to the boat.'

Ilaria obeyed and tugged the cord so that Silvia could grab hold of the side of the boat where there was a rope ladder. She climbed up whilst hoisting a cluster of rubbish with her.

Silvia, back on deck, threw the plastic bag and other rubbish she had collected onto the floor.

'Unbelievable! Every season it gets worse.'

'Where did it come from?' Ilaria asked.

'Who knows, there are so many ships using these waters that any one of them could be responsible. They create so much waste and then just dump it into the ocean.'

Ilaria screwed up her face. 'That's horrible.'

Silvia opened a large storage container at the back of the boat it was full of other rubbish she had collected and she added these new items to it.

'It barely makes a difference but I can't stand to leave these things floating in the sea.'

Ilaria felt sick, she had never witnessed the effect of human wastage before. *We do a good job of hiding the terrible things we do,* she thought.

'We should get people together, to go sailing and collect all the rubbish in the all the oceans,' Ilaria stated with vigour.

Silvia smiled at her. 'If only it were that simple, we would need a thousand ships and twice as many international laws to make any difference. I'm afraid, Ilaria, we are fighting a losing battle between the planet and mankind. The problem in the end is, everyone loses.'

Ilaria wasn't prepared for the tight feeling she suddenly felt in her stomach. It was like someone had taken hold of her insides and tugged on them. It reminded her of being winded as a younger child, when she had jumped off a high climbing frame and kneed herself in the tummy. She hadn't been able to breathe for almost a minute.

Silvia removed her safety rope, getting on with the practical task at hand.

'Right, well let's set our course for the night.'

Ilaria nodded. 'Yes, ma'am.'

Silvia chuckled. They fixed their course and readied the ship to continue sailing along the north coast of Africa. Anticipating a clear, starry night, Ilaria couldn't wait to lay her head back and watch the poems of light, written by the night sky.

'Right, you can take first watch this time. Wake me up in a few hours unless anything out of the ordinary happens,' Silvia said.

'Aye, aye, captain,' Ilaria replied, saluting in a mock military fashion. Silvia laughed at that. She began making her way down beneath the decks as Ilaria kept watch under the speckles of distant worlds that began to sparkle as the last remnants of the sun's gaze fell beneath the horizon.

SEVERAL HOURS PASSED before a ferocious rain began to

pound down on the ship's sails. The material became sodden and heavy and when the forceful wind blew, it sent the sailboat rocking from side to side. Ilaria was soaked from head to toe and had bruised her elbow by falling across the deck, crashing into a storage crate.

Silvia came running from below decks having woken abruptly.

'Ilaria! Are you alright? Ilaria?' Silvia screamed into the storm but by the time her words reached Ilaria they were nothing more than whispers, drowned by the operatic wails of the squall.

'Silvia! I'm sorry, it just came out of nowhere.' Ilaria tried her best to make her way to Silvia but staggered across the decks as she went. Silvia wrapped her arm around a loose rope, steadying herself and grabbed Ilaria tight by her shoulder.

'Are you alright?' Silvia demanded, and Ilaria nodded in return. 'We have to drop the sails or we'll roll right over.'

'Okay, tell me what to do.'

Silvia gave her instructions and the two shipmates ran to the rigging to bring down the sails. It was hard work, as every time they tried to loosen the ropes the wind blew them to the side. After several trying minutes, battling crashing waves and resisting the power of the wind that blew them, Ilaria and Silvia managed to lower the sails and the boat suddenly became more stable.

'We did it!' Ilaria shouted, waving to Silvia across the deck.

Silvia put her thumb and forefinger together, making an OK signal and held up her hand to Ilaria and smiled. 'I can't imagine sailing without you watching my back ever again,

Ilaria. How do you fancy joining my crew?' Silvia said half joking and half meaningfully.

Ilaria was slightly stunned at the offer, not knowing truly if it was one or not. She imagined a life on the open waters as Silvia's right-hand woman. Sailing the Mediterranean and admiring the forces of nature. She felt herself abandon all intention of heading to Tuscany to find the dragon and as if her ancestors rode the storm, angered by her thoughts, a large wave came swooping across the deck and toppled her over. Once the surge had cleared, Silvia was left standing alone. Ilaria was nowhere to be seen.

11

The eye of a storm is oddly quiet and calm. Surrounded by fierce winds and rain and though, in itself, it is relatively safe and peaceful, it remains trapped and encircled by a raging tempest. Such was the nature of Speranza's soul.

His ferocious outbursts had been contained for hundreds of years as he was always bonded to a human, but now the feelings that had lain dormant bubbled to the surface, replacing the kindness and gentleness that had been forged for him.

Traditionally when a dragon's human counterpart was near the end of their life, they prepared their child and the bonding was a seamless transition from mother to daughter, or father to son.

Speranza had been alone now for over a week, his dragon instincts returning to him like a wrecking ball. He had almost forgotten his true nature. A wild creature, the size of a large ship, whose fiery breath needed to be released. He had remained underground these past weeks, breathing his fire ever more fiercely towards the earth's core. He had gone too far and now the dozen or so volcanoes that had been dormant had erupted for the first time in generations. The ash cloud had now grown so thick across most of Italy that the heat from the sun was struggling to warm the earth. Ash had drifted down to the surface and people were finding a thin layer across the tops of their cars. Some had even begun coughing where the ash was at its thickest.

Despite the pleading of the rest of the sect that bonded with the dragons, Speranza remained oblivious to their concerns.

One morning, feeling violently claustrophobic and agitated, Speranza flew through a large underground tunnel at such a speed that he crashed through a seawall, flooding the chamber behind him. He swam joyously through the ocean, rising through the waves and soaring upwards into the sky. He abandoned all caution in being seen above the earth's surface, a pledge he had once made to remain hidden, now broken.

Speranza flew so high that he could see the world for hundreds of miles. A small island to the north caught his attention. It looked so familiar, like an old home now forgotten. But before he could remember why it meant something to him, he spotted a small sailboat, broken in two and shipwrecked on the rocks just off the coast of Palermo. He suddenly felt a surge of breathing that was not his own. A heartbeat in his soul that made no sense to him. He suddenly realised that Ilaria was close by and she was in danger.

Speranza remembered the girl from the dream they had shared. He did not know why but he knew she was important. She reminded him of an old friend, recently lost. Speranza needed to know what was so special about this child that she prayed on his mind and he began his search.

The dragon roared across the ocean, screaming desperately for some sign of life. As he flew, the heartbeat in his mind grew stronger and he began to hear the faintest of cries. Someone was calling out to him to save them. Pleading calls for help.

Speranza swept down across the surface of the ocean. Like a speck of dust lost in a desert, Ilaria remained still and helpless, bobbing up and down in the waves. It was doubtful she could remain conscious for much longer as the freezing cold sea drained the warmth from her body. She looked up into the sky and saw the dragon soaring down towards her.

The next moment was unfathomable. Speranza clutched Ilaria's lifejacket with his claws and pulled her up into the clouds. He saw her pale face as she shivered and so Speranza breathed the softest of warm air onto her. It was like a beautiful summer breeze, except for the stale smell that accompanied it. Ilaria suddenly felt a rush through her entire body and when she opened her eyes, it was not her own vision she saw, but sight through the eyes of Speranza. She shivered as all the energy was whipped right out of her and before she passed out she clutched on tight to the dragon's back, riding not as a passenger, but as one with the dragon.

THERE WERE loud banging sounds coming from another room, pots and pans being stacked against one another and thrown into a sink. The room was dark, the only light a slither of sunlight breaking through the wooden shutters that encased the window.

Ilaria's head was pounding and the noise from the kitchen that awoke her was as offensive a way to be roused as she had known. She tried her best to sit up but her entire body was aching. She had never felt this way before. Her senses seemed heightened somehow and yet her body refused to do anything that she asked of it.

Birds were singing outside and not the faintest drone of a car could be heard. The walls reminded Ilaria of the old Tuscan country houses she had seen in pictures of her grandmother.

Voices were carrying through the house and though she could understand barely a word, she could tell that they were those of a middle-aged couple arguing.

After a short while the pair stopped shouting at each other and the sound of the front door slamming shut downstairs rang through the house. It was not long after that, that a slender middle-aged woman crept into the room where Ilaria lay still and placed a bowl of soup and a piece of bread down quietly before leaving. Ilaria, famished, immediately reached for the bread, which smelt like it had been baked only moments ago. The aroma alone enlivened her.

Once she was done eating, Ilaria lay her head back on the pillow and closed her eyes, drifting off again into a quiet slumber. Wondering if she had dreamed, or if she was still dreaming.

'Buongiorno,' said the calm voice of the woman. Ilaria sat up immediately, her headache still causing her discomfort but her aches lessened now. *How long have I slept?*

'Hello,' Ilaria said. 'Where am I?'

'You are in my home, you are safe now. This place, it's called Chiesanuova. It's a small village in Italy.' The woman had a very strong accent but her English was near perfect. Something Ilaria had learnt about the rest of Europe these past two weeks was that almost everyone spoke very good English.

'How did I get here?' Ilaria asked.

'Don't worry about that, we've got plenty of time to talk. First let's get you strong again. You've been asleep for nearly three days now.'

'What? How is that possible?'

'It takes it out of you, what you did. The first time is the worst, so they tell me. My name is Alice. A long time ago, I was your mother's best friend.'

Ilaria felt nauseous, so overrun by emotions that she didn't even try to stop the river of tears that cascaded down her face. In that moment, she felt closer to her mother than she had ever done. It was as though her presence was in the room and Alice was like an angel, sent to deliver a message.

'Speranza, the dragon, he brought me here didn't he?' Ilaria queried.

'Yes.'

'Where is he now? Why didn't he wait with me for when I awoke?'

'He took a risk coming out into the open, but grazie a dio that he did, or you might have perished in that storm. But something seemed wrong with him, I think he has become too wild again. Do you have the heart fragment pendant?'

'No, I think someone stole it from me back in England.'

Alice hung her head, speechless. Ilaria spoke again. 'This is all my fault, isn't it?'

Alice shook her head. 'No, not at all, none of this is your fault. But we must find that pendant or you will never bond with Speranza and I dread to think what comes next. We better get you up for now, I'll show you around.'

Ilaria was daunted by the prospect that others also wanted her to be bonded with Speranza. It made her feel even more like she had failed. She rolled herself out of the bed and threw on the shawl that Alice gave her. She stretched and let out a very loud yawn that made Alice laugh and Ilaria laughed with her. But that laugh turned to worry as she thought about the ship in the storm and her captain.

'The woman I was with, Silvia. Do you know if she's okay? She was sailing to Sicily with me before the storm hit us.'

'I'm sorry, but I don't know anything. Your boat crashed into the rocks just shy of the port at Palermo but that's all we know. Let us pray Silvia made it out okay.'

Ilaria swallowed a frog. She couldn't bear to think that something may have happened to Silvia and vowed to find her. Somehow.

Timidly, Ilaria asked, 'I heard arguing when I first woke up. Was that your husband downstairs with you?'

'Yes, I am afraid Diego has been a bit upset these last few days. But don't worry, he'll come around eventually.'

Ilaria felt terrible, she remembered being told about Diego before. Her grandfather had once told her about the winemaker who nearly married her mother. The weight of responsibility for his distress pinned against her chest and she hadn't even been conscious during whatever upheaval she had caused.

'He is upset I am here, isn't he?'

'No, of course not. He's just. Well, Diego is Diego. But it is not my place to tell his story. I am sure he can explain himself to you once he's calmed down.' Alice handed Ilaria a pair of sandals and a glass of water. 'You look so much like your mother, you know. Giulia wouldn't believe that we were together now. It brings me joy to see you, Ilaria. Come on, let me show you around. I've been looking forward to giving you a tour of the vineyard.'

Alice led Ilaria out of the room and downstairs into the large open plan living room and kitchen. There was a huge fireplace that was big enough to sit inside and the floor was tiled with terracotta bricks. They went outside and when Ilaria looked up at the ash cloud above her, she felt quite chilly and for a moment thought that a snowflake had landed on her cheek, but instead it was a speck of ash.

'It's so cold,' said Ilaria.

'Yes, this is not normally the case this time of year. I am afraid it will only get worse unless Speranza listens to reason.'

'You mean unless I can bond with him so that he listens to me?'

Alice smiled at Ilaria and then gestured for the girl to follow her as they walked up the stony path that cut through the garden. There wasn't another house around for miles.

'Usually the air becomes very still and humid around now. You get used to sleeping with damp sheets after a while as even the nights are hot and sweaty, but the ash is blocking out the sun and if it grows we will be in trouble. Ah, look here.' Alice led Ilaria down a track between two large fields of grape vines, set on a hill overlooking a forest. 'These are the vines we grow. They would normally be ready to pick in a couple of months and a lot of people usually come here for the harvest. One of Diego's friends, Francesco, is our head winemaker. He assures the quality, along with Diego, and organises the workforce that pick the grapes. But with the way the weather is turned I fear there will be no harvest this year.'

'Maybe it's not too late, not yet! It's very beautiful,' Ilaria remarked. 'What is that in the distance?' she asked, pointing to a large domed building that stood above the sea of clouds along the hazy horizon.

'Il Duomo. That is the cathedral in Firenze or Florence. On a clear day, you can see almost all the city, even from here. We have been coming down here to look at her every day and the more she vanishes, the colder it gets. Come on,' Alice said smiling, 'I have someone I'd love for you to meet.'

They carried on to the bottom of the path where the vines joined the treeline and suddenly a small red animal darted out from behind a tree. Ilaria jumped back, surprised at first, but then stepped forwards cautiously and approached the ginger cat.

'This is Nespola, or Red. She seems happy to meet you,' Alice said as Nespola ran circles around them both.

'She's wonderful,' Ilaria said, stroking the cat who seemed more than pleased with the attention. 'What is a nespola?'

'It's a kind of fruit, medlar you would call it I think. It's the exact same colour as her coat and it grows even in the winter, not very usual for a fruit.'

'She doesn't have a collar,' Ilaria indicated.

'No, she is wild, like most of the cats around here. She travels between one house or another being fed randomly by anyone who happens to be nearby at dinnertime. The rest of the day you will find her here, hunting butterflies and other small animals.'

Alice and Ilaria carried on their walk around the farm. They bumped into a beekeeper who had just pulled a fresh honeycomb from his bee hive. He let Ilaria taste it as he was clearly pleased to show off how fresh it was and without question the honey did taste incredible.

Ilaria fell in love instantly with Chiesanuova as Alice led her into the centre of the village to meet some of the locals. There were only three shops in the entire village. A panetteria which made the most famous schiacciata bread in the whole of Tuscany, a small café that became a bar in the evening that Diego ran on the side of his wine business, and a small café at the bottom of the hill.

They picked up some of the famous bread from the bakery after Ilaria had impressed some of the locals with the couple of Italian words she could speak and walked back up the hill to the villa to prepare the evening meal. To Ilaria's surprise they didn't eat until nearly ten o'clock that evening and her tummy rumbled for hours beforehand.

Alice stirred a huge pot of pasta that she had prepared by hand and told Ilaria of her love of cooking; always with fresh ingredients and never anything frozen.

'Diego should be home soon,' Alice said. 'We'll eat together and you can ask us whatever questions you want. I know you must have a lot going through your mind right now.'

Ilaria certainly did have a lot going on in her head and that was without even mentioning the elephant in the room that was the hundred-foot-long dragon that had recently saved her life.

'Thank you, it's very kind of you to take me in like this. I wasn't expecting it when I set out originally. I assumed when I arrived that I would just go and find a bench in a park somewhere to sleep on and spend days walking around, trying to find someone who knew my family.'

'Don't be silly, we're as good as family. This is your home now as well, for as long as you need.'

Ilaria went a slight shade of scarlet but before she had the chance to thank Alice for the hundredth time that evening, Diego came bounding through the front door and dumped a crate of wine and water. He headed towards Alice and gave her a kiss before dipping his finger in the pasta sauce and tasting it. 'Mmm, buona,' he said approvingly then walked straight to the dining table without paying any attention to Ilaria whatsoever.

Ilaria sighed. It was going to be a very long and awkward evening. After all she had been through, the heartache and adventure, she had grown up and Diego, whatever issues he had, were to do with her mother and not her. She wanted to be his friend and not his enemy. She dished up a plate for him and held her head up high as she went to join Alice and Diego at the dining table and she wasn't afraid. After all, she was the girl who had ridden a dragon.

12

They ran freely through the fields, stepping over the jutting roots of the vines. The early spring sun beat down upon them and as it warmed the earth, a low mist rose from the previous night's damp.

All those years ago they had been the closest of friends; Alice, Giulia and Diego. Never apart for more than a day at a time. After school, they would travel back together on the yellow bus that dropped them a few kilometres down the road from Diego's parents' farm where they now played.

It was a Saturday afternoon like any other in the Tuscan countryside. The three friends loved to play hide and seek amongst the vineyards and forests at the back of the house. Giulia and Alice both lived in apartments next door to each other in the centre of the village and neither of them had the luxury of a garden so they always went to play at the vineyard. The vines had been left to rot as Diego's father had no interest in making wine but Diego vowed one day to bring it back to life.

'Nature is the most important ally we have, and yet we let her waste away like she was a mad old woman seeing out the rest of her days,' Diego said, as the three friends had stopped chasing each other to take a break by the nearby lake.

They dipped their toes in the cold spring water and watched as the ducks swam back and forth.

'It's a lot of work to keep a vineyard in order. I remember what your father explained to us. Maybe you should listen to him too,' Giulia said.

'Listen to him? He wants to sell the land, or lease the fields to other families.'

Alice spoke next. 'Well there is a lot of competition around here. Maybe it's not such a bad idea? What do you know about making wine anyway? Have you ever pruned a day in your life?'

Diego stood up and hovering above the two girls he shouted angrily, 'You're both stupid. I'll bring this place back to how it was before, you'll see. Then you'll both work for me as my servants in the house.'

Giulia and Alice burst out in fits of laughter that only angered Diego more and he dove into the lake and swam away from them.

'Diego! It's freezing,' Giulia cried out.

'Oh, Giulia, what are we going to do with him?' Alice asked.

'I don't know, but I get the feeling he'll bug us for as long as we both live.'

Alice and Giulia stood on the rock from where Diego had dived and jumped in together causing a tremendous splash. Half the ducks in the lake flapped their wings and flew to the far side, nearly crashing into Diego in the process. When he had managed to make his way out of the group of ducks he smacked his hand in the water, cursing at his two friends who continued to laugh at his expense. It was that day, when Diego was just fourteen years old, that he vowed to himself that he would prove everyone else wrong and turn the farm into the best winery in the area.

DIEGO TOOK another sip of wine as he paused from recounting his story to Ilaria. Almost thirty years had passed by since that spring afternoon. She was engrossed to hear about all the mischief her mother had got into when she was not much older than Ilaria was now. Ilaria, still sad, smiled to herself, feeling like she knew her mother a little better now, though it made her longing for her even stronger.

'Thank you for telling me your story, it means a lot to me,' Ilaria said.

'Alice is right about most things. You should thank her. I'm sorry I was rude to you earlier.'

'Sure.' Not allies yet, Ilaria thought. But it was progress. 'How did you come to meet my father?'

Diego scoffed at that question. 'Him. I don't talk about him, you want to know about your father you speak to Alice, preferably when I am not around.'

'Oh, okay.'

Ilaria knew that she had stepped over the line. At least she knew where it was now. Diego continued sincerely, 'Listen, Ilaria, a lot has happened that you do not know, nor are you responsible for. But you should understand that your arrival brings with it a flock of memories that are not always full of happiness.'

Ilaria looked down, ashamed. But then a thought came to her. Diego had spent his childhood and early adult life in the company of her mother who she had never known, so he in fact had a lot to be thankful for. She felt angry then. Was he so ungrateful?

'Fair enough, but I think you should understand something too. I never got to know my own parents, I know them only through the memories of others. I never got to swim in the lake with my mother or learn about farmland from my father. So, let's not pretend that you are alone in suffering.'

Ilaria found herself getting more and more worked up as she spoke. She surprised herself as she hadn't intended on getting upset but after she'd said the words out loud, a horrible wave of confusion came over her and she could no longer bear to sit at the table.

Ilaria got up, leaving half her dinner untouched and went upstairs, slamming the door to her room behind her. Alice stood to follow her but Diego placed his hand on her arm and shook his head.

'Lasciarla in pace, Alice. Give her some space,' he said.

A COUPLE of hours passed by but Ilaria couldn't sleep. Part of her felt guilty for her little outburst, and she felt foolish for being so weak though surely it was justified. Once she had argued fiercely with her grandfather because he had forgotten to collect her from school. She had been right to point out his failing and yet at the same time she couldn't help but feel ashamed at the way she had spoken to him. Ilaria hated her guilt. It was worse than any other emotion she knew.

Ilaria was completely restless so she wandered around the bedroom. There were several bookshelves filled with books that were entirely to do with agriculture. She picked one up to read but couldn't understand the words so she put it back and sat on her bed, wondering what it must have been like to grow up in this village. It certainly would have been a lot easier to pass the time outdoors than in Southbourne. She hoped that one day she would get to feel the Tuscan sun on her face and swim in the lake by the forest. She thought about the ash cloud and reached out, trying to find some sign of Speranza.

Are you there?

Nothing. She didn't understand the connection she had felt with Speranza when he saved her, even without the heart fragment there had been something between them. Then.

You should be resting.

You can hear me? I don't understand.

Stop interrupting me, girl. I don't want you poking around inside my head.

You must stop breathing so much of your fire. I think something bad is going to happen.

Another long silence.

It isn't that simple. Imagine it is as if you could hold your breath for no more than a minute but you were asked not to breathe for an hour.

Ilaria felt her head begin to hurt, and the connection was lost. She filled her mind with other thoughts to clear the dragon from her mind. She thought about Johnny and hoped that his father was okay. It wouldn't be long before the volcanoes beyond Europe began to erupt too, if Speranza carried on at the rate he was.

A knock came at the door and Ilaria threw a blanket over her head to hide, desperately pretending to be fast asleep.

Diego opened the door ever so slightly and quietly spoke. 'Ilaria, I know you're awake, I heard you talking to yourself.' Ilaria felt silly. When had she begun this habit of thinking out loud?

'Come in then,' she said.

Diego crept into the room and sat on a pallet by the side of her bed.

'You remind me of her you know. I am sorry that this causes me pain, when it should bring me joy. I think my own pride sometimes controls me.'

'Why did she leave you?' Ilaria's muffled voice trembled from beneath her blanket.

Diego took a deep breath but found himself surprisingly calm. 'Ever since that day, I told everyone that she left me because I was too busy with the farm. Through my ignorance she had made a friend in an English guy who she met while visiting her grandparents in the UK. The worst part was that I actually really liked him, your father. He was a very decent man. But I pretended that I didn't have time to love Giulia. The reality is, she just didn't love me. No reason, sometimes you either feel something or you don't. We'd been friends for so long I think she was trying her best to fall in love with me, but when she met Christopher she found out what love truly was.'

It was hard for Ilaria to hear her parents being spoken

about in this way. Such a complex web adults weave for themselves.

Diego continued. 'We make up reasons and excuses when other people hurt us in matters of the heart. It is difficult to accept that there is no logical reason. Maybe if I'd spent more time with her, maybe if I hadn't been so busy trying to prove myself all the time I would have noticed I was losing her. I asked myself these questions and hundreds like them for years. None of those things matter in the end.'

Diego took a deep breath and wiped his face with his sleeve. 'I don't think your mother ever forgave me when she told me about your family and the dragons. She took a huge risk by confiding in me and at first I refused to believe her. Then when I did, I told her she was selfish to want to spend so much time working with the other bonded humans.'

Diego stood up from the pallet and turned towards the bundle of blankets that Ilaria was hiding beneath. 'So, now you have heard my confession. Something I never told anyone, not even your grandfather. I love Alice, Ilaria. You must know that. It's just that you have thrown salt on old wounds.'

Ilaria emerged from the sheets and faced Diego. She saw a weary but rugged face before her. A strong and proud man, also arrogant. But he had a kindness in him that had been expressed through his admission that Ilaria would always be grateful for.

'Are you bonded with a dragon?' she asked.

Diego chuckled. 'No, no. They would never allow me to be part of the order. I'm just a friend, who keeps an eye on things for the others sometimes. Everyone knew that you would eventually come here. Speranza told them shortly before Brian died that he planned to bring you here. But he has forgotten himself. It is as though he has fragments of his memory. That's why we need to get to him before there is no human connection left in him at all.' Diego sighed. 'It is incredible that you made it here all by yourself.'

'Well, not quite by myself,' Ilaria replied, thinking about all the help she had had and how she had been carried all the way from Sicily by the dragon. *Was Speranza behind all her good fortune?* 'Thank you for your honesty. Not many people in my life have given me the truth before.'

'Well, you strike me as the kind of girl who won't give up, ever, in the pursuit of the truth. You are a mystery, Ilaria, somehow Speranza has been watching over you, in spite of the fact you are not bonded.'

'He spoke to me. I mean, I heard a voice in my head.'

'That can't be possible. No one has ever spoken to a dragon without being bonded.'

Ilaria was confused; it had happened so effortlessly she'd assumed it was normal. Somehow Speranza guided her and yet his human connection was fading. The hourglass was quicksand beneath her feet.

'You're very strong, Ilaria. Believe me when I tell you, you are going to need that strength. Tomorrow we travel deep underground, to the deepest den. We must find that pendant. A lot of people are waiting there to meet you. It is time that you learnt about this great responsibility you have inherited, because we haven't a moment more to lose.'

13

I laria awoke suddenly, her heart racing. She breathed out and a cloud of mist drifted into the room. For a moment, she thought she was still dreaming. Dreaming perhaps that she was becoming a dragon. But then she realised that the breath was not smoke from fire but an icy vapour and her bed sheets were cold. A gelid cold.

Her skin was a purple shade of blue and she quickly raced to her wardrobe, shivering and numb, throwing on as many layers of clothes as possible.

She ran outside the front door and nearly slipped on a sheet of ice but Alice managed to catch her. The whole vineyard looked like a winter wonderland but with none of the joyfulness. Icicles were hanging from the branches and even the mist in the air looked frozen.

Nespola darted past Ilaria and into the house, searching for warmth, but there was none.

'What happened?' Ilaria asked.

'É veramente grave. Ila. I think we're in big trouble,'

Alice responded. 'We'd better get moving. We'll have to trek through the countryside. Do you have boots?'

'No, I only brought these little shoes.'

'Don't worry, I should have some old ones that will fit you.'

After Ilaria had tripled up her socks to fit into the boots she went to join Diego who was trying to start his truck. The engine was whining but it wouldn't start.

'Dammit. It's useless, we'll have to walk,' he said, before giving the rear of the motor the sole of his boot.

'The entrance is miles away,' Alice said. 'It'll take half the day.'

'We'd better not lose any more time then. I dread to think what is waiting for us down there.'

Ilaria followed Diego and Alice as they grabbed their supplies and walked up the pathway out of the farm, treading carefully so as not to fall on the icy ground.

'Has this happened before? The freezing weather in the heart of summer?' Ilaria asked, hoping that the answer was yes.

'Only once, but not in any of our lifetimes. Maybe before the first dragon was tamed.'

'The first dragon. That was Speranza, wasn't it?'

Alice thought for a moment. 'Yes, exactly. He must have really gone out of control to move your ancestor to track him down and tame him. None of us really know how it happened the first time.'

Ilaria looked down, ashamed. Her first day as a dragon tamer after her grandad had died and she had lost the pendant.

'I wish I'd never been expected to take this responsibility.

It won't do anyone any good.'

Ilaria couldn't get her head around it. Alice and Diego looked at each other and then, trying to reassure Ilaria, suggested that they press on, that the rest of the order would know what to do.

The three companions marched on across the white sheeted countryside. As they passed other villas they saw smoke billowing from the chimneys, the inhabitants desperately trying to create some warmth but with wood supplies that would not last long.

After a few hours, they finally arrived at a small church that sat atop a hill. It was surrounded by acres of land and jutted out from a cliff edge.

'This is it,' Diego said. 'The entrance to the main tunnel. It's too small for the dragons so only humans can use this entrance, but it is the quickest way.'

Diego took a large key and turned it in the lock of the entrance gate and pushed open the large stone door, the metal hinges creaking and groaning. He grabbed a couple of wooden torches from the wall inside. There was a fire burning in a plinth basin in the centre of the room, filled with a kind of slow burning oil and Alice took one of the torches and dunked it into the bowl, lighting her torch and then the other that Diego held.

They continued to the back of the room where there was a small stone staircase that spiralled down into the ground. It seemed to go on forever as they made their way deeper and deeper underground.

Eventually the three came to a tight passageway. They slipped through it sideways as it was too narrow to walk through normally and Ilaria winced as the damp oily rocks rubbed against her. She tried her best to ignore the slime that had attached itself to her arms and once they were through the enclosed path that opened out into a large cavern, she vigorously wiped it off.

'I don't understand,' Diego said, concerned. 'They should be here. This is the first meeting point in case of an emergency.'

Diego ran through the cave, so large in scale that the light from the bright flickering torch he held dwindled into the darkness. Ilaria was scared. Alice took her hand and they walked together through the opening. There were old wooden tables and stools littered around the cave and on the walls were metal brackets where lit torches burned to illuminate the chamber.

Ilaria felt the faintest of touches flutter against her. It was not a physical touch, but one in her mind, yet it still sent tendrils of shivers through her body.

'He's in trouble,' Ilaria blurted out. 'It's Speranza, he is weak and afraid. He's very afraid.'

Suddenly a whooshing sound echoed through the cave and was followed by a dull thud as Diego dropped to the ground. His torch rolled across the stony floor and revealed the features of a lanky creature, hunched over, holding a large club in its hand. Ilaria met its gaze and froze before Alice had time to scream. Ilaria tried to turn and run but before she could she felt a damp cloth forcefully press against her face; the smell of something strange seeped through it and into her mouth and nose. It was sweet and intoxicating. It overwhelmed her senses and suddenly, like a candle extinguished in a storm, it was dark and she was dreaming.

14

A hummingbird is one of the smallest birds. During flight, its heart beats twelve hundred times each minute and even during rest it still beats two hundred and fifty times per minute.

In ancient times, the Aztecs would wear charms in the form of a hummingbird as it was said to give the bearer great energy and talents in warfare. It was even believed that a fallen soldier would return to the world in their next life as a hummingbird.

The intensity of their flapping wings is like the distant vibration of a pneumatic drill. The hummingbird had been Ilaria's grandfather's favourite animal. He had told her of his travels to the Americas during his youth where he had first seen and heard the creature that he was awestruck by.

ILARIA FELT herself floating through passageways, weightlessly. Her heart was racing and she wondered if she had died and been reborn as a hummingbird that was mid-flight. She wondered then if her grandfather had also come back as a hummingbird. He had told her once how they were very antisocial creatures and rarely spent time together unless grudgingly to share in feeding. She didn't care; if they were both hummingbirds now she would find him and they would stay together.

But surely a bird that weighed only a couple of grams wouldn't have felt the same heavy aches of the back and neck that Ilaria was suffering. Her pulse had barely slowed but it was no longer a soft gentle feeling inside her. It was a ferocious pounding that had awoken her from a daze. She felt like she was going to die and yet a strange wave of energy took hold of her, but as she tried to stand her body could hardly carry her weight. To be so fatigued and awake at the same time scared her to the very core.

As her eyes adjusted to the darkness she saw that she was being held captive inside a small cell built into a cave wall. There was an iron gate that separated her from a corridor that disappeared out of view.

A shrieking sound reverberated through the tunnels and carried into the corner where Ilaria had planted herself. It was a horrifying sound. All she had was a handful of straw that she bunched together to try and create a soft base to sit on. The vision of the creature that had sprung out of the shadows and knocked Diego unconscious plagued her mind. She hoped he and Alice were alright. The creature had looked almost the same as the one she had seen in her dream when she had taken back Speranza's heart. But something had been different about the face, almost as though it had been decorated purposefully.

A rattling sound came from the bars that kept her prisoner. Ilaria dare not look up as the metallic clang of keys unlocking the cell rang out.

'Come with me, girl,' said the muffled and abysmal voice.

'Are you going to kill me?'

'That depends.'

Hardly the response she had hoped for, but she clung dearly to any chance of survival. 'Diego and Alice, are they alive?'

The creature groaned. 'For now. Come quickly.'

Ilaria feared greatly for them. If obeying this monster was her only means to help keep them alive, then for now she would follow every command.

She was led down a winding passage, trundling slowly behind the creature. She could hear its heavy breathing as it groaned and wheezed with every breath. It was not long before she was ushered into an opening and Ilaria was startled to find herself inside what looked like a study that formed part of an ancient library. Thick wicked candles were strewn about the place and scrolls were stacked from floor to ceiling, sealed by wax crests. Ilaria recognised the crest on one of the scrolls immediately; it was a hummingbird.

Sitting in front of her was another one of the strange creatures, and she knew then that she had been kidnapped by the heart thieves.

'Sit,' said the heart thief from behind the desk. This one sounded oddly articulate and its voice was less broken. It was almost comforting. Ilaria sat down. 'I suppose you want to know what is going on, girl?'

'Stop calling me girl, my name is Ilaria.' She was getting frustrated now. But she knew she must remain calm.

'Yes I know. Ilaria, the last descendent of the Hope dynasty, the youngest to ever be bonded with a dragon. Except you aren't bonded are you. Because you lost the heart fragment before you even realised you needed it.'

The heart thief placed the pendant on the table in front of them right there and then. Ilaria flushed, wanting to scream *how* and *why?* But no words would form in her dry mouth.

'Where are my manners? Some water?' The heart thief poured a glass and used its elongated fingers to push it across the table towards her. 'Did they tell you everything? Our misguided friends? All the lies, about how you must help keep watch over the dragons and prevent the world from falling into a state that would destroy all life.'

'No, I still don't know anything. Every time someone is going to explain something to me they either die or get clubbed over the head by some cowardly creature, hiding in the shadows.'

'Oh, I see. Well that is unfortunate, but lucky for me I suppose that I get to be the first to tell you who you really are. It's funny sometimes how life works. You plan something for many years and still a revelation that you couldn't possibly have dreamed of will present itself. At least your education will begin with the truth for the first time in our family's history.'

Ilaria felt her heart skip a beat. She didn't like the use of the words *our friends* or *our family*. Was it some trick to scare her? Suddenly she panicked. Had everything she'd heard been a lie? She was an orphan after all. Everything she knew she had learnt from her grandfather. She knew he hadn't been completely forthcoming but he would never have lied to her to that degree, would he?

Had all the memories she thought were real just been stories she had been told that infiltrated her mind in the form of recollections? Had she ever truly known anything about herself. No, her grandfather had loved her dearly. That much she knew was true. As the thoughts buzzed around her head, the heart thief began to remove something that was attached to its face; it was as though tree roots that were growing out of its neck were being prised away. It was disgusting but Ilaria couldn't look away. It spoke again. 'One thing you were wrong about already, Ilaria. The heart thieves as you call us are not creatures or monsters.'

As it finished pulling away the tangled roots and moss and what seemed at first like flesh but was actually densely packed leaves, a human face was revealed. The face of a middle-aged woman. She pulled off her fingers next, these turned out to be damp twigs that concealed her human hands.

The look she gave Ilaria was one of sorrow and pity and confusion. The kind of confusion that only love can bestow.

Ilaria could only bring herself to say one word.

'Mother.'

15

The net was heavy and thick. It had been doused in a sticky substance that smelt like honey. They had never used something like this before. The attack had been planned carefully and for a very long time. The entire retinue of dragon tamers poisoned in one foul swoop. Speranza thought that even for the heart thieves this was a demonic blow to strike. Were they all dead now? There was no way to know, for the plan had worked and once the tamers were out of the way, it had been easy to sneak up on the dragons and cast the nets upon them to steal their magic hearts. Not just one or two. But all of them.

Speranza could hear the faint and tired panting of his friends stuck in other tunnels. He called out to them and all they could do was respond faintly so at least he knew they were still alive.

Speranza tried to wriggle to loosen the net but it clung on tight. It was like a straitjacket designed solely for a dragon. He rolled to the side in an attempt to slacken the underside, which was not connected. It was like a fly flapping its wings whilst caught in a web.

Ilaria, girl, do you hear me? There was no response. One minute he couldn't shake the girl from his mind but now Ilaria would not hear a single thought. He had barely spoken a word to her and ignored her pleading to find calmness. Now that power had been taken from him he cried out with regret, wishing to sense just a whisper of her. He needed help.

TIME PASSES MUCH FASTER for a dragon without its second heart. Partly due to shortened life expectancy. It was all about relativity. Like when a human experiences time as a child the world moves slowly, but when it reaches old age each day passes by as though it were just a fleeting moment. So when a dragon knows its life is to be cut short, those years remaining feel like no time at all.

Speranza felt his anger rising again. Though it was a rage laced with fatigue. He felt the pinprick in his side where a sword was still lodged from the attack. He rolled over as much as he could, trying to dislodge it, but realised that something or someone was lying underneath him. Speranza shuffled backwards as much as the net would allow and saw the crushed creature lying face down on the ground. His memory was hazy but he hadn't remembered killing it.

He shuffled and felt a pain in his side and it occurred to him that his second heart might not have been taken, perhaps it was only dislodged.

Speranza roared out a cry that was heard for miles

through the caves, using all the energy he had, hoping that someone would hear him and come to his aid.

Time passed more slowly now, waiting and waiting. But no one came. Speranza tried breathing a hot flame across the net that snagged against his snout, but the oily, sticky substance that it was doused in seemed to be protecting the layers of rope beneath. Speranza knew he could easily burn through it with the heat of his most severe flames but in his weakened state it was impossible to burn so fiercely. He felt tired again. All he wanted to do was sleep.

Hours went by and it was hard to tell if it was now night or day. He rubbed his head against the side of the cave trying to get comfortable. He was resigned to his fate. Maybe this was how it would end for him. So why not try to get comfortable as he was left to waste away in this tunnel.

It was then, at the moment of his resignation, that he heard footsteps approaching. There was a familiar smell and one that he welcomed, for it was the smell of an ally. Diego approached the dragon carefully. 'I'm here to help,' he said as he placed his hand on Speranza's scaly head as the dragon breathed a deep sigh of relief.

'They've taken her. They took both of them. Ilaria, Alice. I've no idea what they will do. I know they don't mean as much to you as they do to me. But please, I need you to help us.'

Speranza rolled his eyes to the side where the heart thief still lay.

'It's dead,' said the dragon.

'Not it, he. Look closer,' Diego said as he bent down to check the creature, seeing that its face appeared to be cracked. He prised away the roots and beneath it found a human's face. 'It's human. I don't understand.'

Speranza cast his mind back. He cursed his memory. The memory of a dragon. 'They have been concealing their identity for hundreds of years. Think now, have you ever seen a heart thief caught? Killed or defeated?'

'No, we only ever chased them away.' Diego struggled to digest any of this but it didn't change his anger. 'I don't care who they are, they've taken Alice. Ilaria will be in danger too if she is with them.'

'Remove the sword from my side. I think my second heart may still be there somewhere.'

Diego moved down to where the sword protruded and pulled it out sharply by the hilt. Speranza didn't flinch too heavily, though it was agony for him. Diego stuck his hand inside the dragon and grasped for the magic heart. He pushed it deeper inside to the small bony cage where it belonged.

Speranza roared. 'Now run, you know what comes next.'

Diego did know and he hadn't waited around for instructions as he staggered away as far as he could. Speranza's roars flooded the tunnels. The temperature in the caves grew and Diego felt a searing heat against his back so he didn't stop and he didn't look back.

16

There was a drawn-out silence as the revelation sank in. Ilaria had always believed she would meet her mother in her next life or even perhaps one day be startled by the gaze of a street cat that would last just a moment, but would be enough to believe that she was there looking out for her. But it was not supposed to be like this. It was not the result of her hopes or dreams, but of a nightmare. She felt horrified, awkward and confused.

Giulia stood up to move about the room, looking up at all the writings that were stored away on shelves. Occasionally she offered a look back towards her daughter as if she was about to speak, but she never found the words. It was as though the reality of the situation had dawned upon her and she was now as lost as Ilaria.

A faint breeze like a breath blew through the chamber causing Ilaria to shudder and one of the candles beside her on the table went out. Giulia walked over to it and lit it again, and as Ilaria looked up at the candlelit eyes of her mother she found herself feeling something completely unexpected. She hated her. She had been alive all this time and let Ilaria believe she was dead. She had been a heart thief, hunting down dragons and undoubtedly harming their human counterparts.

'Why?' The word slipped out of Ilaria's mouth without even knowing to which question she sought the answer.

'Where to begin, with such a broad question as that.' Giulia scoured the shelves and came across a scroll, which she analysed before putting it back and picking up another. 'Here we are.' She broke the hummingbird seal on the scroll, unravelled the old piece of parchment and began to read.

'The first dragon was tamed by Argentum Spés. It was an oddly cold night in Rome given that it was the heart of summer and Argentum, who had been there on business, travelled alone to an uninhabited island somewhere off the west coast of Tuscany. There had been rumours spread by local fishermen in the town of Castiglione di Pescaia, of a large bird flying high above the marble skies where the island sat. Argentum borrowed a small boat and spent a day and night sailing to the island. He beached up on a craggy rock formation and hiked up a hill, with nothing more than the clothes on his back. The dragon took one look at him and decided that he would make a fine meal but Argentum walked so carefully and thoughtfully towards the dragon that it did not attack, but waited, amused, to see what the tiny man would do. He held out his hand and touched the dragon on his scales, right where his heart would be, instantly creating a bond with it that enabled him to bend its will. Argentum had been a master negotiator prior to this day but there is still no understanding of how he learnt about this magic and it would be a magic that he would pass down for generations to come. From that moment on Argentum convinced the dragon to remain hidden from sight and to sedate the

intensity of his powerful fire breath that was overheating the earth's core. There were over twenty dragons in existence at the time and all of those followed the ways of Speranza. The volcanoes that threatened the land became dormant and the ash cloud lifted, revealing once again, the light of the sun.'

Giulia put the scroll back on the shelf, unsealed. 'The first time I read this scroll, I was not much older than you are now. It was written by one of the old librarians who was alive in the time of Argentum. I think it was then that the first seed of doubt was sown in me.' Giulia took a step towards Ilaria who was in a trance, listening to and watching her mother. 'I didn't believe anything the heart thieves had told me when I first came here. But one day, thanks to my knowledge of its whereabouts, I helped them raid an old vault that stored the history of our family. This library is the result of that raid. Inside these scrolls are the arrogant truths of how the dragons were manipulated by our ancestors. Do you see how they are written, almost as if boasting of their achievements?'

'Why?' Ilaria asked again, hesitating once more to finish her sentence.

Giulia smiled. 'There it is again, your favourite question. Did you know Argentum was from one of the richest families in Rome? They owned most of the farmland around the outskirts of the ancient city, not to mention all around Sicily and of course, Tuscany. Their expansion was being threatened by the unpredictable seasonal weather.' Giulia unrolled another scroll and ran her finger down the parchment to a column at the bottom. 'Here, this is the earliest record of the productivity of the farmer's markets run by Argentum and his children. In the months following his journey to the island to bond with Speranza, his businesses began to thrive. He profited greatly from the more predictable seasons that came about as a result of the dragons sustaining the temperature of the centre of the earth. But at the same time, the youngest and weakest of the dragons died, because for them to breathe fire is like for us to drink water. We may go a day or even two without it but eventually we would die of thirst. If a dragon does not release the scorching heat contained within them, they are consumed by it.'

Disappointment was all Ilaria felt. But could she be so surprised at the greed of her ancestors? They were, after all, a mere reflection of everything she had come to learn about mankind. *And so what if he profited from manipulating the dragon? Did he not deserve some reward for putting an end to the volcanic disruption?*

'But how can that be any worse that stealing the dragon's hearts? You're condemning them to death in a way that is far more brutal and unkind,' Ilaria said, determined to understand.

'Their magic hearts are dangerous and make them more powerful than they should be and it is the dragon tamers who have exploited that power, not us. The heart thieves were also farmers you see, some even used to work for Argentum. But when he had bonded with the dragon, he used his influence to send Speranza on a rampage through the night, burning all the farmland that belonged to those smaller families, eradicating all competition. But you won't find that fact documented amongst these scrolls.'

'But you're after the same thing!' Ilaria exclaimed. 'You and the tamers are both trying to control the dragons, just not in the same way.' She paused, frustrated and confused. 'Is there such thing as the truth?' Ilaria asked innocently.

'Yes, of course, the truth is that you are my daughter. My own flesh and blood. I had you followed and stole the pendant from you. I've whispered in Speranza's ear ever since you got on that ferry, making sure you would come here, because it was finally time for you to know the truth.' She paused. 'Truth, like history, is shrouded in confusion. Like when you see the facade of an old building being renovated. The face paints the picture of a certain period of time, long forgotten. Though it may be true that you get a feeling from it, an indication of that history, behind those walls, the guts have been torn out time and time again. The structures are reformed and new lives are lived. The stories that were once stored behind those walls are rewritten so many times over that the truth becomes a murky puddle where it was once clear water.'

Giulia took the pendant from the table and exited through the library door. 'Follow me, there is much for you to see.'

Ilaria followed her mother through the door, which was then closed and locked with a key that Giulia wore around her neck. They moved on slowly through the winding tunnels that were illuminated by candles. The walls were covered in preserved charcoal drawings from across the ages. The one thing they had in common was that each drawing contained a depiction of families, living in the outside world together, as though they were reminders of another kind of life that took place above the earth's surface before the heart thieves had settled underground.

'We mustn't move too fast through these passages, the

draught our bodies make blows out the flames. There is far less air down here than nearer to the surface.'

Ilaria felt like running and blowing them all out so she could escape but her fear kept her from doing so. *Did she need to be afraid of her mother?* She had created a surrogate for Giulia in her mind. But the woman she was with now was a stranger to her. Ilaria didn't know any more if she was a prisoner or a guest.

'Am I your prisoner?' she boldly asked.

Giulia spun round to look at Ilaria and laughed. 'No, of course not. I'm sorry it must seem that way but you were quite unwell when we brought you here; the cell was a cruel place for us to leave you to rest.'

'Are my friends okay? Have you killed them?' Ilaria blurted it out as she thought how Giulia had no right to pretend she was a friend entertaining a guest, let alone a mother trying to educate a daughter.

At this Giulia stopped walking altogether and placed her hands on Ilaria's shoulders. It was their first physical contact and by all rights ought to have been more awkward, but Ilaria suddenly found herself feeling relieved, like an unknown desire to be held by her mother was being satisfied.

'Listen to me carefully, little one, your friends are all safe. There has not been, nor will there be, any killing as far as I can insist. The dragon tamers, like you, were drugged to make their capture far simpler. But no one was harmed unnecessarily.'

'But I saw Diego get knocked unconscious. He was your friend, and once your boyfriend!' Ilaria shouted at Giulia louder than she had intended and instantly felt embarrassed.

'Diego will be fine, he is one of those people that always bounces back, no matter how often or how hard he is knocked down.'

That sounded slightly like an old lover's rebuke but Ilaria chose to ignore it. Instead she continued walking and asked her mother question after question as they wandered through the underground maze together. They tramped on for what seemed like hours. Ilaria saw many of the other heart thieves resting, playing with their children. There was even a small school they passed where Giulia explained how their existence remained so secret that they could not send their children above ground to interact with the rest of the people who lived there.

Eventually they walked past a series of cells, not unlike the one Ilaria had been kept in. There were dozens of people lying asleep.

'You see, here are your friends, safe and sound.'

'I never even met any of them,' Ilaria said woefully. Everyone was a stranger to her now. She didn't know who to trust or believe. Diego wasn't there but in the very last cell she saw Alice and ran over to her. 'Alice, you're alive! Are you okay?'

There was no response.

'Ilaria, she is resting, she was given a far stronger dose than you were, but I promise we will see her when she is better.' The tone in Giulia's voice implied that she dreaded that moment.

Giulia led Ilaria away from the cells and into a chamber where dozens of people were meeting. It seemed like an official gathering was taking place.

'Look,' Giulia said. 'They are deciding what must happen next.'

'But, don't they have a plan already? Surely you have thought this through.'

'Every single pendant containing a fragment from the dragons' hearts has been taken and locked away. Now we must figure out what comes next. Remember what I told you about truth. We are lucky if we have just a fraction of it. But one thing I can tell you; the time for the tamers using dragons for their own selfish gain has come to an end.'

'So you plan to use them instead? How is that any better? And for what? Some sort of revenge for these farmers? You're not even really one of them,' Ilaria said, devastated.

Giulia took a deep sigh. 'My creed is right action, not the misguided actions of the family I was born into. Ilaria, the tamers are not your creed either. Surely you must see that.'

'I just see two sets of people on either side of an argument. The dragons are stuck in the middle, they're just a tool for you to abuse. If you keep their second hearts they'll die. I dreamed that Speranza would have granted me a wish to save Grandad but in turn the dragon would die. And I couldn't let it.' Ilaria felt lost in the maze of this underground world.

Giulia's expression changed. For the first time since learning of her father's death she began to acknowledge it. 'Another fairy tale, hummingbird. There are no wishes to be granted.'

'How did you know he called me that?' Ilaria asked.

'It was his name for you before you were born. Your father and I took the sonogram to show my parents and when he saw you in the picture of my womb he called you hummingbird. That was a good day.'

Ilaria wanted to cry. She missed her grandfather dreadfully. Gazing around the room at all the heart thieves she began to wonder who these people were. Beneath those disguises were mothers, daughters, fathers, sons and grandparents. People willing to sacrifice their own lives to protect the planet. Even if it meant living as hermits underground, being mistaken for horrid monsters all these years, they had spent their lives, dedicated to this moment. The icy chill that was covering the ground above had been Speranza's doing, and now he was going to suffer for it. But these people had suffered too. It all made Ilaria feel very sad.

'Something I still don't understand,' Ilaria started. 'How did you survive the plane crash that day?'

Giulia had long prepared herself for that question. She tried her best to answer it but as she went to speak a lump lodged in her throat so she coughed. Her admission came next. 'I was never on the plane. I had argued with your grandfather the day before the trip and so the next morning I decided to disappear and leave them alone. Your father and grandmother went on without us but my dad stayed behind, in case I came back. It was that same day that the heart thieves came for me. I fought them hopelessly and wouldn't listen to reason, until eventually I allowed them to explain what had happened and they told me about the plane crash. They allowed me to mourn in peace for several days, though I could not leave. I was shocked to discover that they were human and though I remained their prisoner for a while, they eventually welcomed me as one of them.'

'You fell for their trap and now you lead them?'

'No, there is no leader. We are just a community who unravelled the lies of the powerful and the rich.'

'Why did you argue with Grandad?' Ilaria asked.

Giulia sighed. 'Well, my mother was preparing to hand over the dragon bond to me, but I told her that I didn't want it. It didn't feel right, being in control of such power. So, I decided I wanted to sever the bond. She called me a traitor, that is why the heart thieves wanted me so badly. They must have known somehow that I felt that way.'

'You're a hypocrite. You do want to control them, by taking all the pendants and Speranza's heart.'

'Only to keep them safe. They shan't be used or exploited. Speranza is too strong, it's a necessary sacrifice.'

'That's ridiculous, you'll get greedy. Everyone always becomes greedy in the end!'

It sounded laughable to say out loud. Ilaria knew she sounded like a foolish child at that moment, but it made the thought clearer in her mind.

Ilaria spoke again. 'You left me when I was only a baby, just to fight some stupid cause.'

Giulia looked down, ashamed. 'It's the hardest thing I have ever done. I knew you would not forgive me but I heard that your grandfather had taken you back to England and told you I was killed in the accident. I guess I thought it was for the best that you believed I was gone, until now.'

Ilaria realised then that her grandfather would have known that his daughter was still alive. He must have decided to make her dead in his own mind and so make her dead for Ilaria as well. Another lie. When would it stop, all the lies and deceit? Human beings truly were despicable if they couldn't even tell the truth to the ones they supposedly loved.

Giulia continued her confession. 'I know you will never forgive me, but I always—'

She was cut short suddenly as a panicked man ran through the chamber shouting. It was another heart thief, but this one was delirious.

'He's dead! Luca is dead, the dragon crushed him.'

'Calm down,' shouted one of the gathered party from the centre of the chamber. 'Explain yourself, slowly.'

'I don't know what happened, but after we cast the net, the dragon managed to roll onto Luca's sword, I think it went unconscious as the heart became dislodged but it crushed Luca in the process. I'm sorry but, I ran away and hid.'

It was Ilaria's mother who stepped forwards then to speak.

'Which dragon was it? Please don't tell me it was Speranza.'

The man didn't need to reply, the look on his face was enough.

'Of course it was, and what of the heart? Do you have it?' Giulia sounded more panicked than the man now. But he simply shook his head ashamed.

Then a blinding rage of energy swirled and spun Ilaria like a top, and she fell to the ground.

Ilaria was dizzied by the intrusion but gathered her strength, got to her feet and ran to the corner of the chamber as instructed. All eyes throughout the room focused on her. Giulia looked at Ilaria confused, and for a moment she saw how afraid her daughter was. She felt a great deal of love for her, but then she suddenly realised what was happening.

'Ilaria...' Giulia stepped slowly towards her as the chamber walls began to shake.

'Mum, no, get down!' Ilaria screamed. But before she had finished her warning, Speranza had broken through the ground at the centre of the chamber sending dust and debris flying, covering everyone and everything. The heart thieves were thrown soaring across the hall as boulders cascaded around the room. Ilaria tried to blink the dust from her eyes and watched through a tearful stare as she saw her mother thrust to the side like a rag doll. But before Ilaria could see where she fell, the flames of the candles blew out and her vision was stolen by the dirt that flew towards her like a sandstorm in the night.

17

Darkness can be a comfort at times. When we wrap ourselves up peacefully at night under warm, soft blankets. But when we are involuntarily plunged into obscurity and trapped under rocks and earth, darkness is the scariest place of all.

Ilaria thought how this would be the worst way to die, to starve slowly in a tiny, pitch black corner of a cave. How long would it take? Hours? Days? Surely not weeks. She dare not try and open her eyes as she knew there would be no light to guide her and her face was so covered in dust that it would sting unbearably.

Ilaria tried to roll to her side and, moving her hand slowly, reached out to release her elbow from under her chest. She was pinned down from all sides. She felt a heavy, wet weight on her shin. A boulder was lodged against her leg and it felt numb. She wondered if the wet feeling was blood. Ilaria used her slightly free arm to scrabble around to try and pull herself into a small gap in front of her.

She could barely move, but against her fingertips she could feel a solid object. It was metallic and attached to a chain. *The pendant,* she thought, and stretched towards it to grapple it towards her. Her body hurt but she managed to get a full grip around the pendant and then she felt a rush through her body like a breeze. But not against her skin, within it.

Yes, girl, we are bonded at last. Speranza trampled her mind with the words. Ilaria didn't know how to respond.

Where are you? Ilaria. Are you close?

She wanted to reply but she wasn't sure how. It was impossible to know where he was when he spoke to her mind and every word was exhausting. It was like when the dragon had saved her from the sea, but this sensation was far stronger.

'I'm here,' she shouted as dust poured into her mouth and she coughed.

I can barely hear you, but I think you are close.

Ilaria winced before she tried to speak again. This time she wouldn't use her voice.

I can't open my mouth, it's covered in dirt.

Don't worry, I will find you, the dragon replied, sensing her fatigue.

Ilaria felt the ground shake and fresh rubble fell from the ceiling, covering her legs.

Wait! Stop! The whole cave feels like it is going to collapse.

There was no response but all movement ceased. Ilaria decided to feel her way around the space. She stretched out her arms as best she could and brushed them across the floor and walls. There were large boulders piled up beside her but beneath one of the bigger rocks was a small gap that she might just be able to crawl through. She took a chance and kicked at the boulder on her shin with her free leg, dislodging it. She waited for the world to collapse around her. It didn't.

Ilaria tried to push herself through the gap like a small animal rustling through a smeuse in a hedge but part of her shirt got caught on a sharp corner. She tore the cloth away and threw the small piece of shirt to the side before continuing her efforts.

Each movement was tiny and excruciating as she grazed her knees on the loose gravel. She took a moment to rest daunted by the hopelessness of the task.

Ilaria lay there and relaxed her whole body. She wanted to sleep. But it was then that a strong arm reached out and grabbed her, pulling her towards the small opening.

A deep voice spoke. 'Hold still.' It was Diego. He was alive. She felt him wipe her face with a piece of clothing that felt and smelt like it was soaked with saliva.

'That's gross,' Ilaria said as she opened her eyes and looked up at his worried face. 'My leg is numb.'

Diego helped her clamber to her feet and she felt uneasy. There was a stream of red down her shin where a rock had broken the skin. Diego took a piece of cloth and wrapped up the wound.

'Can you walk?' he asked.

'Yes, I think so. Thank you.'

'Di niente. Let's go.'

They headed out of a passage that had remained open despite the fallen rocks. The rest of the chamber was completely buried. There's no way anyone could have survived that, Ilaria thought.

'Where is Alice?'

A relived response came. 'She is okay, the cells were unaffected by the cave-in. Everyone is waiting.'

Diego led Ilaria out of the heart thieves' den and after a long journey through a myriad of passages they came upon a dozen or more people who were gathered at the edge of an underground cliff.

The opening was like the inside of a cathedral. The earthy ceiling was curved, towering above them. There was a slight crack at the very top, as thin as a knife edge, and just a slither of light beamed through. It was enough to illuminate the whole cavernous space.

The group of people hammered and chipped away at several locked cases. It was fruitless labour. The cases were made of solid steel and old oak that would take days to break through. Diego shook his head, frustrated.

'The thieves locked the dragon hearts and pendants in this case, and we're trying to get them out.' He picked up an old pick axe, observing its worth. *Useless,* he thought.

'Have you asked Speranza? He could open them easily.' Ilaria realised that she was the only one who could talk to the dragon when he wasn't present so she closed her eyes and held the pendant tight and focused her mind. She was incredibly tired but this was important.

I'm free. We're in a large chamber. You must come quickly and open these boxes so we can give the dragons back their hearts.

A moment of silence.

Then.

I'm on my way.

Then, in the next moment, a panicked woman came running towards Ilaria. She wrapped her arms around her. Ilaria hadn't had time to see who it was but she knew it was Alice who embraced her.

Alice spoke first. 'I'm so glad you are alive. Did they hurt you?'

Yes, they had, but not the way Alice thought. 'No they didn't hurt me,' Ilaria lied. 'Alice, my mother was there in the chamber, along with the other heart thieves. They are people, just like us.' Her voice was pleading, as if preparing Alice to find forgiveness.

'That's not possible, your mother died years ago in the plane crash.' Alice shook her head. 'I'm sorry, but I don't know who that was that you saw.'

'No, I'm telling you, it was her. I know it was.'

Diego moved closer to Ilaria to try and talk some sense into her. 'Ilaria, I know you are in shock, but I'm afraid Alice is right. You're still recovering from the poison that they gave you.'

'I'm not in shock,' Ilaria argued. 'You've seen them now, they are people.'

'Yes, I know. It was quite a surprise to us too, but I am afraid your mother is not amongst them.'

'We have to find her!' Ilaria was screaming now. 'She could still be alive under the rocks.'

Diego slumped his head, not knowing how to win this argument. He didn't have to.

Seconds later Speranza flew up from the bottom of the cliff edge and perched next to the gathering of people who moved back to give him space.

The dragon lifted his front claws and crushed the cases

like they were wicker baskets. A dozen shiny green objects poured out of the remains and the people began to gather them. Suddenly the earth began to shake as a chorus of dragons flew up the cliff edge to perch on the ridge. Each had come to claim their second heart. They appeared to be gasping, as though fatigued.

But they were magnificent. Ilaria had thought she would be used to the idea of dragons by now but nothing could have prepared her for the impact of seeing a dozen of them standing side by side. They roared in unison as they retook their hearts and together they flew back down to the bottom of the cliff and vanished. Only Speranza remained behind.

With a flash of amber light the temperature of the cliff top rose and fire burst up from the cavernous opening like a winter wave breaking against a rocky beach. The gathering moved back to keep away from the searing flames and cheered once they were at a safe distance as the inferno danced before them.

I'm sorry I didn't listen to you before, I endangered so many people. But now the broken bonds can be rekindled.

The voice in Ilaria's head sounded proud. But something dawned on her then and she ran to Speranza who lowered his head to her and she placed her hand on his snout.

'No, they mustn't be,' she said. 'Tell them they are free now.'

There was a commotion amongst the gathered crowd. One of the dragon protectors came forward to speak. 'Young girl, we must be re-bonded with the dragons. It is our only chance to protect the world.'

Ilaria turned to face the gathering and responded with a calm voice. 'It's funny. Whenever a human says they want to save the world, they mean they want to save mankind. The world would be better off without mankind.' Ilaria turned back to Speranza. 'We've been using you for so long. It's not right. We have ruined this world and you have lost your freedom because of how selfish people are.' She thought of the scroll from the library. 'You remember him, I know you do. Argentum Spés, my ancestor. He forced you not to breathe your fire anymore, and many of your kind died. Then he used you to destroy the farms of other people. Those people are the ones you all call the heart thieves.'

For the first time in hundreds of years Speranza was silenced. His giant scaly-lidded blue eyes looked sad, like a distant memory had come back to him and it caused him pain.

Argentum.

Yes.

I remember him.

Of course you do, he was the first. And I will be the last.

And with that, Ilaria took her own pendant, and all the others that had been stolen from the case and she threw them into the abyss beyond the cave's edge. She felt the breeze rush through her again and then it was gone, she had severed her connection with Speranza. She knew it had worked because when the dragon looked at her she knew he spoke to her mind but she heard not a whisper.

'Ilaria!' Alice shouted. 'What have you done?'

Ilaria walked up to Alice sympathetically and wrapped her arms around her waist. Alice embraced her. 'Oh, child, what have you done?'

Ilaria began to cry. If it was guilt she felt, she didn't care. She sniffed and buried her head into Alice's jacket like the lost girl that she suddenly felt she was. All eyes were on her as Speranza flapped his gargantuan wings and disappeared. Shock and despair filled the air around them like a sea mist settling on a quiet beach. Ilaria was the one who spoke.

'No more lies.'

18

Snowflakes and ash flecks interspersed, drifting towards the hilltops where a cloaked gathering stood waiting. Their blankets and scarves billowed in the wind as the frost gripped them like prison shackles. They were captives of the cold that enveloped them, a bitter cold, biting, severe and fatal.

Ilaria wondered what they were waiting for. There was a certain acceptance that all the pathways that had been open to them were now closed. Yet despite that, Ilaria could not get her mother out of her mind. It seemed so foolish to be worried whether she were still alive under those rocks. She couldn't help but be angry that no one else believed she had seen her mother, considering they were all probably going to be dead before the next sun rose if the temperature continued to drop so rapidly. The damage had been done, even if the dragons had remained bonded and held back their fiery breath; too much ash had now formed in the sky, surely?

The group remained huddled together in a tight formation, occasionally taking it in turns to move towards the centre, which was the warmest place to stand. Alice and Diego remained close to Ilaria for fear of her safety amongst the throng.

Diego pointed to a small crater that sat in a valley beside the abandoned church they had entered previously. 'You see that lower patch of snow over there?'

Ilaria nodded.

'That is where they will leave from.'

'How long does it take…' Ilaria had to pause for a moment, as the end of the question that had been on her mind for so long suddenly seemed so hard to say out loud, 'for a person to freeze?'

Alice shook her head and sighed. 'We're rafting down rapids blind now.'

A blow to the heart. Ilaria felt it worse than the cold. Alice hadn't forgiven her for severing the connection with Speranza. But she sensed a certain selfishness in the tone of Alice's voice. Maybe that was the same desire to live that had caused Argentum to become so selfish, or the heart thieves to want to steal the dragons' hearts. But it hadn't been that desire to live that had caused her mother to remain dead to her all these years. That was a sacrifice she had made, for something she believed in that was bigger than herself.

'If what you say about your mother is true—that she became a heart thief—we could have worked together. Our goal was the same, and now both heart thief and tamer alike have failed.' Alice felt a small tear roll down her cheek before it froze. 'We were all too blind and greedy to work together. In the end it was nothing more than a battle between rich and poor.'

Ilaria took Alice by the hand, trying in her own way to give her comfort. 'I know you blame me for what is happening. I'm sorry. I guess I am a heart thief too.'

'No,' said Diego. She sensed pride in the words he spoke next. 'Ilaria, you are something else entirely. Neither heart thief nor a tamer. You are the heart giver. The first of her kind. You did what no one before you could have even conceived of. Not driven by greed or a selfish need to live. You set them free, whatever that might mean.'

Ilaria felt a shiver go down her spine and she couldn't tell if it was because of what Diego had said or because of the dozen dragons that suddenly burst through the snow-topped soil beside the old church, soaring upwards into the air. They twirled and dived as though they were swimming and the sky was their ocean. It was the first time they had truly been free for a thousand years.

They flew off into the distance towards the western coast. Back to the island where Argentum had first travelled to bond with Speranza.

Alice couldn't help but draw a smile. 'Where do you think they will go?'

Ilaria knew the answer to that. 'They are going home.'

SOME TIME HAD PASSED since the flight of the dragons. The old tamers felt alone and despair began to weigh in on them.

'Well, at least we die together. Like a family,' said one of them.

Another replied. 'We *are* family, in a way we always have been.'

'Do you think they will remember us? Many years from now, when human beings are a distant memory and dragons are rulers of the earth?'

It was said with some disdain. Ilaria didn't blame the man but she thought how only human beings felt the need to conquer and rule. The dragons probably didn't even want to be rulers; surely they only wanted to live. She thought about rebuking him but decided against it. *Why poke a hole in a sinking ship?*

A breeze fluttered across the hilltop and they all felt it in their bones. There was a tawny light in the sky that cast a glow on the whiteness of the countryside surrounding them. Very little daylight remained and the night would bring a ruthless kind of cold that none of them would survive. If the ash they choked on didn't take them first.

'Shouldn't we get to shelter?' said one of the more fearful of the group.

No one could see what good that would do; there was no escaping what was approaching them. 'Each of us is free to do as they wish, but I'm staying here,' Diego said.

From a great distance a dot appeared in the sky. It was coming from the direction that the dragons had flown towards. Ilaria broke from the group and walked across the hilltop to get a better look. The dot became a larger shape like a bat, flapping its wings slowly and powerfully. A roar came from the approaching bird-like creature, but it was no bird. Ilaria heard Speranza in the cry that echoed across the valley. She wondered if he had come to say goodbye.

The earth shook as he landed in front of Ilaria and he wrapped his wings around her and breathed a warm, gentle breath into the enclosure he had created. It was a wonderful feeling.

'Why have you come back?' she asked.

Speranza blinked affectionately with his eyelids. 'I remembered that day, when Argentum came to me. I remember now, thinking how he'd taste delicious and how insignificant a creature he was. His race to me meant nothing, merely a snack to satisfy a moment of greed. I realise now that he was just the same as I was. But he was not insignificant, despite his intentions; hundreds of years would pass and then there would be you. Maybe mankind has run its course, maybe this is a new beginning. But you have altered the path of my kind, Ilaria. Your very existence provides a strong case for your kind to live. As you have allowed us to.'

Ilaria was confused. Surely Speranza knew that it was not possible for them to survive this cold. 'There is no hope for us, but it is comforting to know you care.'

'Hope is exactly what there is, Ilaria. Hope is standing right in front of me. You must promise me, never to change. Humans have lived upon the earth for tens of thousands of years. We have been here for far longer than that. It shouldn't be a choice between one or the other. We can learn to contain our wildness. I don't know if it can happen overnight, but we can try. But people must learn to control their greed or we will all suffer. Humans can be kind and thoughtful—you have proven this much to me—and with your help they will find a way to undo the damage they are causing to the planet. My dearest child, we have work to do.'

Speranza lifted his wings and stood up high and without saying another word he soared up into the air.

'I don't understand, what is he doing?' asked Alice.

Ilaria felt optimistic but also afraid and guilty. 'He's going to save us.' She knew then that she had a lifelong bond with the dragon, not one of manipulation or trickery. But one of genuine trust and appreciation for each other's existence, a chance to live in harmony.

She knew what she was compelled to do, find a way to improve the earth. That meant changing the desires of her own kind. It was not a one-person job, that much was certain.

Ilaria had never wanted her mother more than in this moment. She thought of her family; her grandfather who had raised her and a grandma she could barely remember. Her father who had loved her mother fiercely. Alice and Diego who had become as close as family to her, and her mother who had taught her the most valuable lesson of sacrifice.

Ilaria smiled and found strength as a warmth tickled her face. The frozen mist in the air began to disperse and a thin layer of snow across the hilltops began to turn to water. The sky lit up with a series of fierce flames rolling above the clouds and it began to rain. Glimmering in the fading light of the sun, the drops trickled down Ilaria's face and as she opened her arms and looked up to the sky, she saw Speranza casting an inferno across the horizon, vaporizing the ash cloud until the blinding light of the solar rays warmed them. A moment later, the entire retinue of dragons were flying above them. Burning off the ash clouds for miles around them, there was no hiding them now. They had brought back the summer and as a final ball of fire rippled across a Tuscan peak, Ilaria gazed at its beauty and searched for her friend, Speranza, who flapped his wings and then he was gone.

19

It had been a long and emotional farewell. Saying goodbye to Alice and Diego was harder than expected but Ilaria knew that she would visit them again soon. She had invited them to travel back to Southbourne with her but they had too much to take care of in the coming weeks.

The airports had reopened after the clouds of ash had dispersed. There had been reports of large animals flying in the sky off the west coast of Italy, breathing fire that broke through the clouds, but all the newspapers had eventually dismissed the idea as a rumour started by some crazed citizen trying to get rich by selling the story.

Work had begun to repair the damage that the volcanic lava had caused across the world. Some people had lost their homes, but thankfully no one had been hurt.

Ilaria missed Speranza. From the brief time they had spent together, there was a part of her that would now be forever changed due to their bonding and she had struggled to transition back to her old life. But Ilaria was grateful to see Johnny and Nawal again and after a long hard discussion, she agreed that she needed to go back to school. That was the hardest part of all. Ilaria didn't mind the foster home she had been placed in. In fact, Mr and Mrs Bishop were incredibly friendly and their fascination with gin was most amusing to Ilaria, as she would often find the pair of them giggling on Friday nights after she finished her paper round, a new job she'd taken as she was saving up to travel back to Italy the following summer. Sitting in a classroom listening to the drivel of her teachers, who Ilaria was now convinced had less clue about life than she did, was frustrating, but she was determined to persevere because she didn't want to disappoint anyone and deep down she knew she had a lot still to learn.

Scott got up to his usual tricks during the lunch breaks and after school but Ilaria had learnt to deal with him non-violently now by showing up his stupidity in front of his friends and after a while, having been humiliated in front of his gang several times, he had given up with Ilaria and Johnny and moved on to his next victims.

On the weekends, Ilaria would sit and read history books and anything else she could find to do with the effects that people were having by using up the resources of the world. Everyone had been so concerned with the volcanic eruptions, they had been completely ignorant to the fact that something called global warming was becoming a real problem. It was evident that most human activity was bad for the environment, damaging the atmosphere with carbon emissions, filling oceans with waste and killing the marine life in the sea. On land, animals living in forests were displaced as trees were torn down to create palm oil or other products that seemed completely unnecessary to Ilaria. She had actually got into an argument with a classmate who had come to school covered in make-up, totally unaware about the damage her *products* were doing. Ilaria's frustration had fallen on deaf ears. Why her class weren't taught these things in school was a mystery to her.

Ilaria had read about a big meeting at a United Nations summit, where almost all the countries of the world had gathered to discuss how to reduce the pollution they were causing. Ilaria had found articles from leading newspapers of several different countries, where the sole focus was aimed at reducing human waste. How pleasing to hear that people seemed to care, she thought, though after further investigation Ilaria realised that they were all lying to each other about what they planned to do and in the end, it was all about political relations, money and power. It was daunting and Ilaria knew she had a very long road ahead of her if she was going to fix anything at all.

Johnny's father had agreed to help Ilaria put up flyers around Southbourne, trying to encourage people to recycle materials that could be reused. He had returned home and found a new job in London so he could be with his family every weekend. Johnny was pleased by this, as he spent most weekends bored now, whilst Ilaria was busy, burying herself in her books instead of hanging out with him. She still saw him at school but wouldn't apologise for ignoring him because *revolutions are not built off the back of play* as she had quoted to him, patronisingly one afternoon.

Time passed by very quickly and before she knew it Ilaria was celebrating her thirteenth birthday. Nawal threw a lovely party for her in the afternoon after having taken Ilaria to the cemetery to visit her grandfather's gravestone. Ilaria's one regret when she had run away was that she hadn't been at his funeral. She was told it had all gone well and most of the residents from her old street had come to pay their respects. Her grandfather would have been very humbled by that, she thought, and before they left she had placed a carving of a hummingbird beside his gravestone.

A SERIES of party poppers went off and confetti filled the air and everyone cheered. Ilaria found herself thinking about how much waste these poppers would create but she tried to ignore that, just for today.

'Happy Birthday, Ilaria,' they all said in unison. Nawal, Johnny and the Bishops were all present, plus a few of the locals from down the street and one or two of Johnny's new schoolmates she had invited. Ilaria laughed heartily at them as they had begun stuffing their faces almost immediately after they arrived.

Ilaria cut her cake, handed out a slice to everyone, and sat joyfully watching them all eat. It reminded her of Christmas spent with her grandfather, whom she credited for her love of breaking bread with others.

Mrs Bishop pulled an envelope out of her purse. 'Oh, Ilaria, a letter arrived for you. They redirected it from the school.'

Ilaria took the letter and couldn't contain her excitement. Had her mother found her somehow? Had she survived the cave-in? Ilaria ran into the next room to get some privacy and tore open the envelope and pored over the letter.

It wasn't from her mother. However, a huge smile spread

across her face as she read it. It was from Silvia, her kind shipmate, who had bought a new boat from the insurance payout for the last yacht that had crashed in the storm.

Ilaria was so happy to hear that she was alright. She had given a forwarding address so that Ilaria could write back to her and tell her of all her adventures. She desperately wanted to take out a pen and begin writing her reply instantly but Johnny burst into the room looking for her.

He asked curiously who had written to her and told her that everyone was looking for her downstairs.

Ilaria told him that one day she would tell him the whole story but she knew he would not believe a single word and so the two friends returned to the party; it was the most time they had spent playing together in months and it brought Ilaria immense joy.

She looked around at all those who had gathered to celebrate her birthday and thought, T*his is worth fighting for*. This moment that she would cherish for the rest of her life. She closed her eyes tight and took a mental picture, so as never to forget.

EPILOGUE

A full moon beamed down on the hot and dry summer's night. In the month that had passed since Ilaria's birthday, she had written to Silvia several times. It usually took about a week to receive a response and when she had read Silvia's reply, expressing her sympathy about her mother, Ilaria had wept.

As she lay in bed, staring at the undulating light across her ceiling, Ilaria waited impatiently, fidgeting, as she couldn't sleep for her excitement. Each hour that passed felt like days and there was nothing she could do to help fill the time. She had packed her bags the previous evening and written all her farewell letters. Johnny had been given his instructions of exactly how and when to hand them out. He wasn't sure about aiding and abetting a runaway—the consequences had been bad enough the last time she had run away and he hadn't had anything to do with that saga—but now he was directly involved. After voicing his concerns, Ilaria simply told him not to be such a sissy.

Ilaria peered out of her window with a view of Hengistbury Head. The rocky mound, filled with muddy, carroty crags, was a beautiful silhouette against the moonlight that reflected off the sea and Ilaria thought how she was going to miss the view from her bedroom as a ray of dawn light came into view. She picked up her bag and threw it over her shoulder, crept to the window and slid it open gently so as not to wake anyone.

As promised, Johnny had snuck out in the night and leant his father's ladder up against the outside of the house for Ilaria to climb down. Once she had jumped off the last rung, Ilaria gave him a huge hug before heading off down the street. She turned and waved to Johnny, who was already dismantling the ladder for fear of being caught, and laughed.

Down by the beach, waves were lapping up against the side of the yacht and Ilaria couldn't contain her excitement as she called out to her skipper.

'There she is,' shouted Silvia from the decks of her new sailboat.

Ilaria ran aboard and embraced Silvia. 'Thank you so much.'

'Of course. What kind of friend would I be if I didn't offer to help you look for her?' Silvia ran her fingers through Ilaria's hair.

'It's not just that. Thank you for believing me. I don't know if we'll find her but just believing that it was all real means so much to me.'

'Of course it was real, and with the journey we have ahead, you have plenty of time to tell me all about it.'

Ilaria nodded and beamed a large grin at her skipper and

went to untie the rope from the jetty the boat was secured to.

They set off into the morning light and this time no storms met them on their voyage. The two friends spoke of everything that had happened. But more than just that, they spoke of everything that might yet come to pass. Seeing the world from the ocean again gave Ilaria a sense of optimism. The endless expanse of water where thousands of creatures lived. The innumerable islands they sailed past, each with its own distinct character. The diverse cultures that they met as they docked in each port to load up supplies, and how Ilaria loved to hear the different languages and dialects. One of her favourite places they visited was the island of Malta, where she loved the friendly locals and the fresh food they ate there. Ilaria did her best to learn at least a few words of every different language she came across. Each one was so unique and colourful and somehow seemed to reflect the way people behaved.

Ilaria knew the world truly was a wonderful place and she was lucky to be a part of it, and as they approached the shores of Tuscany, she cast her gaze to the south where one special island existed beyond the horizon and for a fleeting moment she thought she saw a dozen shadows floating across the vermillion sky.

A WORD FROM RICHARD

Thank you for reading book one of The Time Thief series. I hope it was as enjoyable for you to read as it was for me to write. The story will continue soon with part two: The Spirit Thief.

I would like to acknowledge and thank Anthony Swingle, Janet Swingle, Mhairi Underwood and Melanie Underwood for their contributions to this book.

There are always exciting updates coming through my author newsletter so why not subscribe to receive exclusive content, freebies and a behind the scenes look at my stories by visiting www.richardaswingle.com

I would love to know your thoughts, so please consider leaving a review on Amazon or Goodreads. This also helps spread the word about my books and enables me to continue writing more stories so you'd be making this writer very happy indeed!

facebook.com/raswingleauthor

twitter.com/raswingle

instagram.com/raswingle

ABOUT THE AUTHOR

Richard A. Swingle is a British fantasy novelist from Brighton, in the UK. This is his second publication, part one of *The Time Thief* series. He comes from a background of working in the Film and Television industry and has been actively writing since the age of fourteen when he discovered his passion for storytelling through making short films.

Since then he has developed his storytelling interests as both a musician and novelist and continues to work as a director of photography in the film industry.

Visit: www.richardaswingle.com to find out more.

Other Publications:

HARMION SERIES

Harmion
The Vermillion Isles *coming soon!*

THE TIME THIEF SERIES

The Heart Thief
The Spirit Thief *coming soon!*

Internal illustrations by Janet Swingle

Cataloguing in Publication Data is available from the British Library

ISBN 978-1-9161170-2-0 (B-format)
ISBN 978-1-9161170-3-7 (Kindle eBook)

www.richardaswingle.com

Printed in Poland
by Amazon Fulfillment
Poland Sp. z o.o., Wrocław

52385411R00101